HARLEQUIN® Presents·

Fantastic Stories for Fall!

Emma Darcy is back with *The Playboy Boss's Chosen
Bride,* the story of arrogant Jake Devila and Merlina,
who grabs her chance to make him see that she's not
just his dowdy, reliable secretary. Penny Jordan is on
sizzling form with *Master of Pleasure*: Sasha thought
she'd walked away from Gabriel Cabrini, but now
he possesses her once more. Julia James guarantees
dark desire in *Purchased for Revenge*: Greek tycoon
Alexei Constantin has only one thing on his mind—
vengeance. If that means bedding Eve he'll do it.
Jane Porter delivers drama, glamour and intense
emotion when Spanish superstar Wolf Kerrick
claims Alexandra, his rags-to-riches bride, in
Hollywood Husband, Contract Wife. For a touch of
regal romance, choose *The Rich Man's Royal Mistress,*
the second part of Robyn Donald's trilogy,
THE ROYAL HOUSE OF ILLYRIA. Virginal Princess
Melissa falls under the spell of man-of-the-world
billionaire Hawke Kennedy. In Elizabeth Power's
compelling *The Millionaire's Love-Child,* Annie and
former boss, Brant Cadman, are reunited in a marriage
of convenience when they discover that their babies
were swapped at birth. While Anton, the Comte
de Valois, demands that Diana become his bride
when she becomes pregnant. But what is behind his
proposal? Find out in *T...*
Bride by Catherine Sp...
the sheikh—the explo...
Prince Malik and Abbie...
marriage into one of Ea...
At the Sheikh's Comm...

He's proud, passionate, primal—
dare she surrender to the Sheikh?

Feel warm winds blowing through your hair
and the hot desert sun on your skin
as you are transported to exotic lands....
As the temperature rises, let yourself be seduced
by our sexy, irresistible sheikhs.

If you love our men of the desert,
look for more stories in this enthralling
miniseries coming soon.

Available only from Harlequin Presents®.

In November:

Bedded by the Desert King
by Susan Stephens
#2583

Kate Walker

AT THE SHEIKH'S COMMAND

Surrender To
The Sheikh

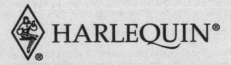

HARLEQUIN®

TORONTO • NEW YORK • LONDON
AMSTERDAM • PARIS • SYDNEY • HAMBURG
STOCKHOLM • ATHENS • TOKYO • MILAN • MADRID
PRAGUE • WARSAW • BUDAPEST • AUCKLAND

ISBN-13: 978-0-373-12576-0
ISBN-10: 0-373-12576-3

AT THE SHEIKH'S COMMAND

First North American Publication 2006.

www.eHarlequin.com

Printed in U.S.A.

All about the author…
Kate Walker

KATE WALKER was born in Nottinghamshire, England, and was the middle child in a family of five girls. She grew up in a home where books were vitally important, and she read anything she could get her hands on. Even before she could write she was making up stories. But everyone told her that she would never make a living as a writer, so she decided that if she couldn't write books, at least she could work with them by becoming a librarian.

It was at the University of Wales, Aberystwyth, that she met her husband, who was also studying at the college. They married and eventually moved to Lincolnshire, where she worked as a children's librarian until her son was born.

After three years of being a full-time housewife and mother she was ready for a new challenge, so she turned to her old love of writing. The first two novels she sent off to Harlequin were rejected, but the third attempt was successful. She can still remember the moment that a letter of acceptance arrived instead of the rejection slip she had been dreading. But the moment she really realized that she was a published writer was when copies of her first book, *The Chalk Line,* arrived just in time to be one of her best Christmas presents ever.

Kate is often asked if she's a romantic person because she writes romances. Her answer is that if being romantic means caring about other people enough to make that extra-special effort for them, then, yes, she is.

Kate loves to hear from her fans. You can contact her through her Web site at www.kate-walker.com, or e-mail her at kate@kate-walker.com.

For The Hoods and everyone in the
Writing Round Robin who made
those weeks such fun.

CHAPTER ONE

IT WAS the outriders that Abbie saw first. Big powerful men on big powerful motorbikes, engines purring, chrome and black gleaming in the sunlight. In spite of the heat, their muscled bodies were encased snugly in supple black leather, their heads concealed in helmets. But then of course these men were the bodyguards of a man who ruled a country far away. A desert country where the sun beat down day after day, building to temperatures far higher than the moderate heat of an English summer's afternoon.

The man who was in the car behind them.

The convoy swept down the drive in a roar of engines, swirling to a halt outside the main door and waiting, bodyguards sitting taut and tense on their machines, unseen eyes clearly darting everywhere, watching, observing. Their job was to protect the occupant of the vehicle that followed them. That big, sleek car with smoked glass windows behind which she could just detect the form of Sheikh Malik bin Rashid Al'Qaim. The car also had a small flag on the bonnet.

The flag of Barakhara.

Abbie drew in a deep breath and felt it tremble all the way into her lungs.

So he was here. It was really happening. This was not a dream. It was absolutely, totally real. And that reality turned it into the biggest nightmare she had ever known. Her grey eyes blurred briefly with tears and she blinked them away hurriedly, pushing trembling hands over the blonde smoothness of her hair as she fought for control.

He was early. They hadn't been expecting him for another half an hour or so. That was why she was still tidying the room, her white blouse and neat skirt covered by the ridiculous cotton apron, splashed all over with big colourful flowers, borrowed from the housekeeper to keep herself clean.

'Dad!' she called, her voice as shaken as her breathing. 'They're here.'

But her father was already aware, already heading out of the room, hurrying into the hall, pulling open the big front door. Abbie saw him pause to draw breath for a moment, brush his hands down his sides to ease their dampness and her heart constricted in fear.

If her father, a man who had always seemed able to handle anything, felt nervous then the worries that had kept her awake at night ever since the news had broken were even more justified than she had feared.

'Good luck!' she called, knowing he would need more than luck.

The whole family would do everything—anything they could—to help Andy. But when her younger brother's fate was in the hands of an absolute ruler of a foreign land, the sheikh of an Arabian country... She had no idea at all what he might demand of them.

He might listen to pleas for leniency, they had been told. Then again, he might refuse to do any such thing. No one, it seemed, could predict the way he might jump. But today, after three weeks of careful negotiation and diplomacy, somehow they had prevailed on this man, this sheikh, at least to discuss the matter with them.

And he was the man inside the car.

The man who...

Abbie's thoughts stopped dead as the uniformed chauffeur now came to the rear car door, opening it smoothly and stepping back, head up, spine stiffened as if at attention. He didn't actually salute, but his whole stance was one of respect and formality as he held the door so that the occupant of the limousine could emerge.

'Oh…'

It was all she could manage. The single syllable escaped from her on a long breathy sigh, pushed out on a wave of shock and pure disbelief. If a sleek black panther had uncoiled itself from a sitting position and prowled out of the car and on to the gravel driveway leading to the house, she couldn't have been more stunned.

Or more afraid.

This man was every bit as big and dark and sleek and powerful as a hunting cat. His long body held a controlled strength that was belied by his easy stride, every lithe movement smooth and relaxed.

But his face was anything but relaxed.

Just looking at his expression sent a cold shiver of dread slipping down Abbie's spine. It was not a pretty face, nor even one that she could describe as handsome. It was too strongly carved for that, all angles and hollows. High, slanting cheekbones defined the forceful lines of his features, emphasising the lean planes of his cheeks, the power of his jaw. There was an aquiline slash of a nose and under straight black brows were the deepest, darkest eyes that Abbie had ever seen.

It was a strong face—a harsh and imposing face. And it was very definitely an unyielding sort of face. Which wasn't something that held out any chance of hope for the help that they needed right now. He was younger than she had anticipated too—closer to thirty than the fifty she had somehow expected. Though whether that was good or bad—a point in their favour or against it—she had no way of guessing.

'I thought he was a sheikh!' a young voice said from close

at hand and looking down, she saw that her youngest brother, George, had come to stand beside her, staring out of the window at the important arrival.

'He is, love. The Sheikh of Barakhara.'

'But he's not wearing the right sort of clothes!'

'No…'

A faint smile touched Abbie's mouth, warming and easing a little of the anxiety from her grey eyes. At just twelve, George was still young enough to think in the simplest terms. Their imposing visitor was a sheikh and, as such, he should be wearing the flowing robes that were the traditional dress of men from his country. Instead, this sheikh was dressed in an immaculate steel-grey silk suit, superbly tailored, hugging the width of straight shoulders that had no need of extra padding to make them, or the chest beneath them, look broad and strong. The fine material slid over the powerful muscles of long, long legs, clung to the lean line of his hips, as he moved forward to where her father now stood on the doorstep, waiting to greet him. Under the afternoon sun, hair black as a raven's wing gleamed glossily sleek and the hand that he lifted to brush it back from his wide forehead had the same smoothly golden bronzed tone as the skin on that devastating face.

'So he's not a real sheikh?'

'Yes—yes, he is, sweetheart. But I think he only wears those robes in his own country.'

'In the desert—when he's riding on his camel?'

'Yes, I expect so.'

Another wider smile curved her lips at her young brother's innocent questions.

'So he is a real sheikh—and he can help Andy?'

Abbie's smile vanished, evaporating rapidly at this reminder of just why the Sheikh was here, and the seriousness of the situation that had brought about his visit.

'Yes, George. I hope so. I really hope so.'

'Daddy will talk to him,' George asserted.

'Daddy will talk to him,' Abbie echoed.

But her voice didn't have the conviction she wished for. Her shadowed eyes were watching the scene beyond the window, seeing the way that the Sheikh strolled towards the door, handsome head held arrogantly high, keen dark eyes scanning his surroundings assessingly.

He held out his hand to her father courteously enough and the clasp seemed firm and sure. But watching James Cavanaugh intently, sensitive to every move, every change of expression, Abbie saw the way the older man almost bowed, instinctively inclining his head in respect for his royal visitor. The gesture worried her. It made her fear that her father had been overawed by this much younger man. She didn't want to think about the possible implications of that.

They needed her father to be fully in control of the situation. He had to be able to cope, to discuss the matter calmly and confidently. Andy's future depended on it.

The thought of her brother, only just nineteen, alone and afraid, locked away in one of Barakhara's darkest, most secure jails made her shiver in fear, her nerves tying themselves into tight, cruel knots in her stomach. Andy had been foolish, stupid, totally irresponsible—but he wasn't *bad*. He'd made a mistake—a very serious one, admittedly, but a mistake was all it was. And if he was given a second chance...

He *had* to be given a second chance! After all, that was why the Sheikh was here.

Surely he wouldn't have travelled all this way just to tell them that he wasn't prepared to show her brother any leniency?

Leaning forward a little, she tugged slightly at the fall of the elderly lace curtain that shielded the window, twitching it aside so that she could see more clearly. Then froze as the small movement caught the corner of the Sheikh's eye, causing him to turn his head sharply, narrowed eyes hunting the source of the distraction. In a heart-stopping second the black, black gaze locked with silver-grey—and held.

'Oh, help!' Abbie couldn't hold back the exclamation of something close to horror.

If she had been a small scurrying mouse that had suddenly looked up and found itself the centre of the concentrated attention of some hunting hawk the shiver of apprehension that raced through her couldn't have been any more fearful. Abbie felt her throat close on a spasm of pure panic and her nerveless fingers let the curtain drop as she stepped back sharply, dodging out of the firing line of that laser-like scrutiny as quickly as she could.

But even so she felt the burn of his gaze hot on her skin, the sense of shock and bewilderment lingering as the net curtain fell back into place, shielding her once again from those sharp, assessing eyes.

Dear God, please let these negotiations be over and done with soon, she prayed silently. For no logical reason whatsoever, she was suddenly assailed by the feeling that she would not be safe while this man was in the house.

She just wanted him to go—be on his way—and out of her life for good.

And yet…she admitted as she stepped back as far out of sight as possible.

And yet she had never seen a man like him in her life. In spite of her fears, she knew that she would find it impossible to erase the image of his stunning features that was etched onto her mind.

If only they could have met some other time, in some other way.

Who the devil was that?

Sheikh Malik bin Rashid Al'Qaim wasn't a man easily distracted from his purpose. If an issue demanded his attention, it got it—wholeheartedly. And the subject he had to discuss with James Cavanaugh was one that needed whole-sale concentration. But, just for a moment, the sudden flash of movement, the twitch of a net curtain over to his left had caught his eye. He had turned...

And found himself transfixed, his gaze caught and held by the blonde who was staring at him in open curiosity from the ground floor window.

A stunning blonde. Tall and slim, with sleek, smooth hair and a figure shapely enough to distract his attention even further just for a moment. Even the ridiculously old-fash-ioned and unflattering cotton apron wrapped around her and tied tightly at her slender waist couldn't disguise the very sensual appeal of the feminine curves it covered.

Curves he would like a closer look at. Very much closer.

But even as the thought crossed his mind the blonde's eyes widened in something like embarrassment and she stepped back hastily, letting the lace curtain drop between them once again, concealing her from him.

No matter.

Malik crushed down the sudden twist of disappointment, the murmur of protest from senses that had been woken by the swift glimpse of the unknown blonde. He had more im-portant matters on his mind. The woman—clearly a maid or some other home help that the Cavanaughs employed—would keep.

'Would you care for something to drink—some refresh-ment after your journey?'

Swiftly Malik turned his attention back to what James Cavanaugh—Sir James Cavanaugh, he reminded himself—was saying.

'That would be very welcome,' he acknowledged and allowed himself to be escorted into the cool shade of the big oak-panelled hall, their footsteps echoing on the ornately tiled floor, his bodyguards following behind him.

He would much rather state his business and get the whole

thing out into the open so that they each knew where they stood, he reflected as he followed the older man through a door on the left and into a large bay-windowed room. A room that had obviously once been elegant and luxurious, but which now showed every sign of the sort of neglect and decay into shabbiness that came from a lack of ready cash to put things right.

He had spotted these indications of disrepair everywhere on the approach to this house. The ornate wrought iron gates had not had a coat of paint in years and were rusting and falling into decay, the fountain in the courtyard was coated in green moss and the flower beds were obviously unweeded and uncultivated.

The house itself might be huge and elegant, showing the way that this family had once held power and status in English society, but clearly the upkeep of their stately home was now beyond the means of the very limited income they possessed.

Which would make his task easier, he decided, watching his host fuss over his comfort in a way that did little to conceal the way that James was clearly a bundle of nerves. They would have little choice but to accept the offer he was here to make, and be grateful for it.

Malik just wished they didn't have to go though this pantomime of welcome and polite small talk first. The friendliness his host was now displaying would vanish soon enough. James Cavanaugh was not going to like what he had to say—not one little bit.

But if James wanted to see his son again this side of young Andrew's fortieth birthday then he would have no alternative but to agree to the conditions he was being offered.

Whether his daughter would go along with them was quite another matter.

CHAPTER TWO

IT WAS like waiting for the countdown to an explosion, Abbie told herself as she headed up the stairs to change, moving as quietly as possible past the library in the hope of hearing what was being said behind the closed door. But the only sound that came through the thick wood was the muffled murmur of voices, too blurred to make out any words, let alone decide how things were going.

She could tell which was her father's voice and which their visitor's but that was all. The rich, accented tones of the Sheikh's words carried even if their meaning didn't—and it appeared that he was doing all the talking.

Which seemed terribly ominous, she admitted, the thought draining all the strength from her legs so that she had to force herself to keep moving, holding on to the carved wooden banister for support. Had her father run out of things to say already? Or had the Sheikh rejected every suggestion put to him and was now laying down the terms on which he would help them?

Or, worse, was he making it plain that he had no mercy to offer? That her brother must serve out the sentence that had been passed on him, without any hope of remission?

'Oh, Andy!'

Bitter tears of despair burned in Abbie's eyes and, as she reached the half-landing, she sagged against the wall, covering her face with her hands.

Her brother had been a delicate child. He suffered badly from asthma and had often been in hospital or just sick at home. As a result he'd missed a lot of schooling so that he was young for his age and very naive. The trip to Barakhara had been his first experience of being abroad on his own. Now he was locked in some foreign prison and in the single brief phone call they had had from him, arranged with a lot of difficulty by the British Ambassador, he had quite obviously been terrified, begging them to get him out—to let him come home.

Frantic diplomatic efforts had followed and the Sheikh's visit was the result of that. It was their only chance. It couldn't fail. It just couldn't!

The sound of movement in the room below jolted her upright in haste. Someone was coming to the door—opening it.

Her father appeared in the hall below. He paused, looked back at the man inside.

The Sheikh, Abbie reminded herself. The man of power who held the future happiness of their family in the palm of his hand.

In the palm of his arrogant hand, a spark of defiance added, recalling the way that the man had turned to look at her in the moment of his arrival. The assessing way those dark eyes had scanned her.

'I'm sorry, but I must take this call.'

It was her father who spoke, his voice floating up to where she stood.

'I won't be long…'

He hurried off in the direction of the kitchen and Abbie watched him go. From her position here, higher up on the landing, even her father's powerful figure looked shortened, smaller somehow and reduced. The sight of him wrenched at Abbie's heart, making her bite her lip hard against the distress that threatened to choke her.

'Oh, Andy...' she began again, then caught herself up sharply.

It wasn't all Andy's fault! Okay, so her brother had been silly—downright stupid—but surely what he'd done hadn't been all that bad! Other boys his age had done as much, worse even! In England, pocketing some items from the archaeological dig he was working on would just be petty theft—wouldn't it? So what right did this sheikh have to lock her brother up and throw away the key?

Anger made her heart swell. A sense of bitter injustice made it beat at twice the speed as before, sending the blood coursing through her veins so fast that it made her head spin.

Who did he think he was? How dared he...?

She hadn't even realised that she was moving until she found herself halfway down the stairs again—heading in the direction of the hallway and the room her father had just left. She didn't know what was going to happen, had no idea what she was going to say. She only knew that she was going to say *something*.

The library door was still partly open, just as her father had left it. There was nothing there to make her stop, or even pause to think. The impetus that had taken her down the stairs had built up into almost a run, taking the last couple of steps two at a time, and sending her hurtling into the room before she had a chance for second thoughts.

Or before she had a chance to think of anything to say.

So there she was, suddenly face to face with the man—the *sheikh*—who had come to make demands of her family. Who was, in most respects, holding her younger brother to ransom, and was now letting them know just how they would have to pay.

Here she was, face to *gorgeous* face...

Oh, no, heaven help her, she didn't want to think of how stunning he was close up. How devastatingly dark and sexy. Just seeing him scrambled her thoughts until she had to fight against the urge to say something that was the complete opposite of the anger that had brought her in here.

He was lounging comfortably at his ease, damn him, in one of the big, well worn, soft leather armchairs that flanked the big open fireplace. His handsome head leaned comfortably against the studded leather back, soft blue-black hair brushing equally soft chestnut leather. His long, long legs were stretched out in front of him, crossed at the ankles, revealing superbly crafted handmade boots. One hand held a teacup, the finest bone china looking absurdly small and delicate, impossibly white, against the burnished bronze strength of his broad palm, the powerful fingers of the other hand resting negligently on the arm of his chair, totally relaxed.

Unlike Abbie, who was fizzing with rage, bristling with defiance.

'You can't do this!'

The words burst from her before she had time to consider them or even try to decide if she would be wiser to hold them back. And she didn't know whether to feel a sense of near panic or intense satisfaction as she saw the way that his head went even further back, forceful jaw tightening, gleaming jet-black eyes narrowing sharply as he looked up into her face.

'I beg your pardon?'

It was a shock to realise that these were the first words she had ever heard him speak clearly. She had been intensely aware of him, of his presence in the house, ever since that moment that he had stepped out of his car and into the sunlit courtyard. It was as if he had always been in her life, not just newly arrived in her experience.

'What did you say?'

The rich, dark, lyrically accented voice had sharpened, developing a razor's edge that made her wince inside to hear it. And there was a new tension in the long muscular body that no longer lounged easily in the chair but had developed the tightness of a coiled spring, like that hunting cat she had imagined earlier waiting and watching for just the right moment to pounce.

He hadn't actually moved but still there was enough of a threat of danger in him, in the tautly drawn jaw, the sharply narrowed eyes, that made her insides quail at the thought of that coldly reined-in anger turned on her. And yet somehow the new sense of risk added a sharper edge to the harsh male beauty of his face, the brilliance of those glittering jet eyes.

But not enough to curb her tongue.

'You can't do this! You can't treat people this way!'

'And what way would that be?'

'You know only too well!'

'I think not.'

To her nervous horror, he was leaning forward to replace the cup and its saucer on the table, uncoiling his long body with a slow and indolent grace as he got to his feet. Standing at his full height, he towered over her, big and overpowering, sending her throat into a spasm of shock and freezing her runaway tongue into silence. She swallowed hard and fought for the control not to turn and run straight for the door—fast!

'I don't believe I know what you're accusing me of—or why,' he went on, the beautiful voice shockingly soft and warm. Deceptively so because there was no way that the tone of his words matched the fierce, cold assessment to which those black, black eyes were subjecting her. 'So perhaps you'd like to explain.'

He'd wanted to meet the sexy blonde from the moment he'd seen her watching him from the window, Malik reminded himself. In fact, he'd agreed to James Cavanaugh's suggestion of tea largely in the hope that the maid would be the one who would bring it. He'd been disappointed when James himself was the one to go and fetch the tray. But then his host had been called away to an important phone call and now here was the blonde, appearing unexpectedly in the library without warning.

He would have sworn that, in the moment their eyes had met earlier, he had seen the same sudden flare of interest, of attraction, that he had felt for her. In fact, he had been so sure of it that he had been content to wait, believing it was only a matter of time before they came together. And her sudden appearance seemed to have proved him right.

She was even more stunning close up than he had imagined from the quick glimpse he had had of her through the window. She was tall, with rich, full breasts, a neat waist and curving hips. That ridiculous apron with its multicoloured flower print should have made her look anything but glamorous but the way it fastened around the slenderness of her waist emphasised the swell of her breasts, the flare of her hips. A real woman, unlike the almost boyish figures of so many of the females he had seen around London.

The sudden clutch of sexual hunger he experienced, just looking at her, was so primitive it was shocking. It was a long time since his rather jaded appetite had been stirred so strongly.

But her mood was not at all as he had anticipated. This hissing, spitting cat had little in common with the image of a warm, willing temptress he had built in his mind, letting himself consider that perhaps this trip to England might not be the boring diplomatic duty and family responsibility it had promised to be.

Instead he was faced with an aggressive, fiery creature who had marched up to him in a way that no woman in Barakhara would ever dare to do, confronting him with her hands on her hips and a blaze in her cool grey eyes.

'I don't need to explain! You know why you're here!'

'My business here is with Sir James—'

The attempt to squash her, silence her, failed as she drew in a sharp breath, then launched into a further attack, dismissing his intervention with an audacious wave of her hand.

'Your business here is to decide Andy's—Andrew's—fate!' she flung at him. 'I don't know who you think you are, dicing with people's lives like that! Just what gives you the right…'

'The law gives me the right,' Malik broke in on her with a snap. 'The law of—Barakhara. The same law that young Andrew chose to flout when he decided to pocket some of the items he found at that archaeological dig he was working on.'

Andy, his mind had noted, grabbing at the single word and working on the meaning behind it. She'd changed it pretty hastily to Andrew, but *Andy* was what she'd said at first, before she'd corrected herself.

And *Andy* meant a familiarity, a closeness that was more than servant to a member of the family she worked for.

'A few paltry items!' she scorned. 'What? A coin or two? A fossil? And for that you'd lock him up for life!'

'A few paltry *religious* items,' Malik corrected coldly. 'Items of deep significance to the history of Barakhara and its rulers. Items that in just the last century would have meant death for any non-Barakharanian to touch…'

He watched the colour ebb from her face with grim satisfaction. The ashen shade of her cheeks told him all he needed to know.

'You didn't know that?'

She could only shake her head, sending the pale gold of her hair flying as she did so.

Andy. Malik's mind went back to the word in the way that he might worry at a sore tooth with his tongue. *Andy*… So what was the relationship between these two? Did they have something going between them? Was *Andy* perhaps her lover? The sting of jealousy that thought brought was as jagged as it was unexpected, making him move sharply, uncomfortably.

'So he omitted to tell you the full facts about why he was arrested?'

Or was it the father who had done that? Was it the truth of the matter that James Cavanaugh—*Sir* James Cavanaugh—didn't want the world to know just what his stupid elder son had been up to?

Malik's mouth curled in distaste. The Honourable Andrew Cavanaugh was what the son called himself—what he had insisted on being called, Jalil had said. And the *Honourable* Andrew Cavanaugh lived in a house like this, with maids to clean and fetch and carry for him, and still he stole to line his own pockets. There was little that was *honourable* about that.

'So now perhaps you'll admit that I have a reason for what I'm doing. That I am not quite the spawn of the devil you think me?'

'I…'

She didn't seem able to find an answer for him. Her soft pink lips opened, but no words would come out. And clouds of confusion dulled the silvery grey of her eyes.

Suddenly Malik felt a sense of rage at the fate that had brought him here, the job he had to do. Why couldn't Jalil do his own dirty work?

There were times when he wished he could just let his young fool of a half-brother go to damnation in his own way. But if Jalil fell, then the whole of his country would go to rack and ruin too, and he had sworn an oath to his mother—Jalil's mother too—that he would never let that happen. A vow made within the family was sacrosanct, and he couldn't live with himself if he didn't keep it—no matter what it took.

He had hoped that a little dalliance with the blonde maid would at least provide some entertainment, some relaxation after the delicate negotiations he was going to have to handle. But from the stubborn, mulish expression on her face, he was going to have to work harder at winning her over than he had ever thought.

The unwanted and uncomfortable thought suddenly hit

him that if she knew the son—this *Andy*—so well, then maybe she was close to the daughter as well.

That was a complication he could do without. He had seen no sign yet of the Gail that Jalil had talked about, but if she and this girl were friends…

'No—he didn't tell me,' she managed now, stumbling over the words faintly and a raw colour washed those pale cheeks, betraying her embarrassment…

And making her look damnably sexy. It might be mortification that had put the blush on her skin but it made her look as if she had just got out of bed after a long, passionate session of sexual indulgence. It might have been the way that she had bitten down hard on her lower lip that had made it so pink, with all the blood rushing to the surface, but in his mind he knew that her mouth would look like that when she had been kissed senseless, taken to ecstasy and beyond.

'What's your name?' he demanded suddenly, his voice rough with the effort of trying to distract himself from the heated blood that seemed to be pooling low in his body, hardening and tightening so that it was a struggle to think straight—to think at all.

'I'm Abbie,' she told him, looking a little startled that he should ask.

Not Gail, Malik thought on a rush of relief. Just for one uncomfortable moment he had wondered…

'And what should I call you?'

She'd pulled back some of her confidence now, some of the strength there had been in her in the moment of her arrival in the room. There was a definite edge of sarcasm to her tone on the question. One that tugged a smile at the corner of his mouth, one that was impossible to hold back.

'You can call me Malik.'

'Malik…' Abbie's tongue curled around the exotic sound of the word as if she were tasting it.

It sounded rich and exotic, strong and firm—just right. Just like him.

'Is that all?'

Her voice was softly husky, dragged from a throat that was too dry, too tight, to speak naturally. She swallowed hard and slicked a moist pink tongue over suddenly parched lips, watching his black gaze drop just for a moment to follow the tiny revealing gesture. And when his eyes lifted again, burning straight into hers, she knew that she was lost. She had fallen into sensual slavery without knowing why or how it had happened. But she was in and tumbling head over heels into an endless chasm of awareness, one from which she already knew she had no hope of escape.

Not that she wanted to. That smile had rocked her world. It had only been a small curl at the corners of his sexy mouth but it had made her shiver in instant reaction, heated pinpricks of awareness tormenting her sensitised skin.

'Shouldn't I add something else?'

Her question brought those brilliant eyes swiftly back up to her face, locking with her own bemused gaze, holding it fixed.

'Add something?' he asked, the musical sound of his voice coiling round her senses like warmed silk. 'Like what?'

Like what? Abbie asked herself, scrabbling through the disorder of her thoughts, trying to find the original track they had been running on, the one she had meant them to follow.

'Like—like *sir*,' she managed hesitatingly.

He was a sheikh, wasn't he? A ruler. Of the royal house of Al'Qaim. Surely he must have some official title that she had to use.

'Or—or *Your Majesty*—or…*Highness*—'

The words broke off, her voice cracking as he moved suddenly, coming so very close. In spite of the heat, she found that she was once again shivering as if a cold draught had blown over her skin.

Having looked into the dark depths of his eyes, she found she couldn't look away again but was held frozen, mesmerised, captive. She couldn't have moved away if she'd tried. But she didn't try—couldn't try—didn't *want* to try.

Instead she knew that the saving grace of all that anger was deserting her, evaporating in the warmth of that smile. And when she saw the faint golden glow of amusement that lit those amazing eyes then she was lost. All the resistance in her melted like ice before a fire.

'Just Malik…' he murmured. Somehow he had moved closer so that the heat of his breath on the words brushed along her cheek, stirring a tendril of hair at the lobe of her ear.

She inhaled deeply, breathing in the scent of him, the warm musk of his skin, and let her breath out again on a sigh.

'Malik…' she said softly, her tongue savouring the exotic sound of his name. The frantic beat of her heart had slowed, become heavy, indolently sensual, and the honeyed warmth of arousal was uncoiling low down in her body, all that was most feminine in her reaching out to all that was masculine in him.

'Malik…' she said again, wanting to say so much more but not having the courage to do so.

Touch me! she wanted to say. *Let me feel the heat of your skin on mine, the strength of your hand, the stroke of your caress…*

But the words died on her lips; she couldn't make her tongue form the words even though she felt as if they were screaming inside her head. She had never felt this way before in her life.

No—the truth was that she had never known that it was possible to feel this way. To know this hunger, this desire for a man she had only just met. A man who made her heart thud, her pulse race, who made her aware of him in every part of her body so that her breasts stung and heat pooled in the most intimate spot between her thighs.

She'd had boyfriends in the past, but no one—*no one*—had ever affected her like this.

'You're beautiful…'

Malik moved slightly, coming even nearer, and once again the scent of his skin, the faintest hint of the perfume of cedar wood, reached out to surround her, tormenting her senses. She couldn't take it any more. Couldn't bear just to stand here and know he was so close—and yet not close enough.

She *had* to touch.

Throwing caution to the wind and giving in to the primal need that made her skin burn, her bones ache with need, she reached out a hand at last…

And encountered *his* hand reaching for her at the same time.

Their fingers met, touched, and it seemed to Abbie that sparks flew in the air, fizzing between them like fireworks. But then those long bronzed fingers tangled with hers, twisting together, holding tightly, drawing her closer to him with an irresistible strength. Abbie knew she had to give in to the need that swamped her, dark waves of sensuality breaking over her head as she almost fell against him and his mouth came down to claim hers.

The kiss that Malik had been imagining since the moment he had first seen her was far more in reality than it had ever been in his mind. The soft feel of Abbie's lips against his own was like setting a match to the tinder-dry brushwood of the hunger that was just waiting to burst into flames, flaring savagely through the whole of his body, making him burn with need. The taste of her on his own mouth, his tongue, was like the most potent aphrodisiac, driving him to plunder the soft interior as she opened to him, yielding in the same moment that she demanded more.

And he would give her more. He wanted this woman so much it was like a thunder in his head, pounding at his thoughts, obliterating all sense of reality. He forgot where he was and why he had come here, the mission he had set out to achieve. All he could focus on was the soft, feminine body in his arms, the tender mouth that opened under his, the hands that clung…

'You're beautiful…'

Her fingers were making a path up his arms, stroking their way over his shoulders, tangling in his hair. The faint scrape of her nails over the sensitive skin of his scalp made him drag in a raw, shaken breath before crushing her closer, taking her mouth yet again. His own hands had found the elastic band that fastened her long blonde hair back and tugged it loose, tangling hard in the silken strands, holding her just so—so that he could kiss her exactly the way he wanted to.

And *she* wanted it too.

There was no resistance in her supple body, no stiffening or drawing away; instead, she pressed closer than ever, the fine bones of her pelvis cradling the heat and hardness of his erection. Each tiny movement she made stoked the fire of need, making it flare higher and hotter and fiercer than ever before.

'I want you…'

He barely recognised his own voice, barely understood the language he spoke, it was so hard and thick and rough with the hunger that tortured him. His accent was harsher than ever before and for a moment it crossed his mind that she might not be able to make out a single word he had spoken.

But the woman in his arms simply sighed and muttered something against his mouth, something so muffled and indistinct that he was forced to wrench his lips away from hers. He tugged her head back with his imprisoning grip on the blonde length of her hair to look down into her passion-flushed face, seeing the sensually glazed eyes, the swollen mouth.

'What?' he demanded, needing to hear the words in spite of the evidence his eyes were giving him. 'What did you say?'

'I said...'

But she didn't even trouble to finish the sentence, reaching up instead to fasten one arm tight around his neck and drag his head down to her again.

'Yes...'

It was a sigh against his mouth again—or a moan. A sound of surrender? A sound of demand?

He didn't know and he didn't care. This wasn't a time for words, for talking, but for action. And the action that his hotly aroused body demanded was that he take this willing and wanton woman hard and fast—and *now!*

With his mouth still on hers, his hands locked in her hair, he half walked, half carried her backwards, moving awkwardly, stiff-legged, supporting her in his arms, dodging furniture by instinct rather than sight until they came hard up against the wall with a thump that drove the breath from her body on a gasp that went straight into his mouth.

Swallowing down the shaken breath, Malik cupped her face in both his hands, tilting it again to get just the right angle to kiss her hard and long, taking the sweetness from her mouth and feeling it intoxicate his already fizzing senses, heat his blood even higher.

'Yes!' he muttered against her lips. 'Yes! You're mine. I knew that from the first moment—'

The words broke off, raw breath rasping in his throat as he felt her hands push between them, tugging at his tie, pulling it loose at his neck, her fingers seeking the warm flesh beneath, raking it hungrily.

'Abbie...' Her name was just a rasp, a sound, barely a real syllable of a word.

'Malik...' Her voice was no better. It shook on his name, coming and going like an untuned radio. 'Malik...'

He crushed her against the wall, unable to get close enough, to feel her warmth and softness against every part of his body. He wanted to spread her out beneath him, to tear her clothes from her body, to feel her heat and tightness enclose his aching sex. But at the same time he didn't want to move away from her for even those few seconds it would take to get them both into that position.

Moving would mean ending that delicious pressure of body against body, heat against heat. It would mean breaking away from the hungry, demanding caress of her hands, the way that her fingers fumbled and snatched at the buttons of his shirt, seeking out the flesh beneath, tugging lightly, tormentingly at the curls of dark hair she found there.

But *he* had to touch *her*. Just the caress of her mouth, the feel of her body beneath the thin cotton blouse, was nowhere near enough. He needed—yearned for—the sensation of skin on skin. Of hot flesh burning into flesh, the heady perfume of arousal reaching into the air and stimulating already strained senses to breaking point.

'Abbie…'

With a rough movement he jerked her into a slightly different position, holding her captive against the wall as he brought his hands down over her thighs, reaching out and grabbing the hem of her skirt, pulling it roughly upwards, rucking it over her hips, exposing the soft skin of her legs.

The soft *bare* skin, he noted on a sound of surprised satisfaction, feeling the silky smoothness beneath his greedy fingertips. Just skin, not the appalling synthetic scratch of tights—just skin, soft as heated velvet, enticing as hell. Just *Abbie*.

And *just Abbie* was all that he wanted.

Her hands had found his skin, buttons were wrenched open, his shirt pulled out of the way until it was skin on skin at last and a sigh broke from her on a gasp of contentment. Her fingers smoothed over his chest, tangling for a brief moment in the curls of body hair before that wandering touch curved over his shoulders, finding the tension in his muscles, then slid down his back, along each vertebrae as far as she could reach.

And Malik needed to touch too. The pressure and heat of body against body just weren't enough. A pressure and heat was building inside him too, rising to boiling point, creating a sensation inwardly that was like some violent volcano that was about to blow. And he would explode if he didn't touch her.

Muttering thick-tongued endearments in his native language, he pushed the clinging skirt even higher. The feel of his fingertips on her hot flesh sent sensations like the shock of a bolt of lightning right through him and he felt the shudder that shook her. The same shudder that tormented his own hungry body.

He heard her moan softly—or was it his own voice he heard? He had no idea but the next moment his mouth captured hers, plundered deep, but then was wrenched fiercely away when just to kiss no longer satisfied. He needed to go further, explore deeper, taste more of her. And she understood totally, arching her neck into his caress, mutely inviting him to take what he wanted.

'Yes…'

It was a sound of yearning, of encouragement, of pure need. One that made an answering need kick hard at him low down in his body.

The ridiculous apron was always in the way. Fastened tight around her waist, about her neck, it hindered every move he tried to make. But by throwing it upwards from below, he had access to the heated core of her. To the lilac-coloured, flimsy bit of nothing that guarded the centre of her femininity. The frivolous bit of silk was such a contrast to the severely practical and sensible outerwear that it brought a shaken laugh into his throat, making him catch his breath in shocked response.

'So this is what you have hidden away under this absurd uniform. This is what the real woman wears. I like it—more than like it.'

He could feel the heat of her even from this distance, feel the moisture that betrayed her hunger. The scent of her aroused body filled his nostrils, obliterating all thought, driving him wild.

And her kisses drove him wilder. Fierce, urgent, demanding little kisses that pecked at his cheek and neck like an insistent, hungry bird. Her hands didn't seem to know where they most wanted to be—in his hair or over his shoulders or down his arms. The jacket he wore was skimmed off, dropped to the floor, discarded carelessly. More buttons were wrenched undone, his shirt was tugged from his waistband, her fingers…

Oh, by Allah, her fingers were unstoppable, probing lower, seeking, touching, caressing…

'Abbie,' he groaned, but whether in encouragement or in protest at the impossibility of actually doing anything *here* and now, he didn't know. 'We can't. We must— We—'

But a wild shake of her head denied his words, not giving him the chance to continue.

'Kiss me,' she demanded. *'Kiss me!'*

He would do more than *kiss* her! So much more!

Her breasts were tight against his chest, the hard points of her nipples communicating the sharpness of the arousal she made no attempt to hide. He wanted to get his hands on those richly curved mounds, to touch—to feel—to taste…

But first he had to get past the bib of that damned apron. The appalling flowered cotton was there between him and what he wanted so much—but not for long! With a muttered curse he wrenched at it, pulling hard at each shoulder. The thin cotton straps snapped without much difficulty, ripping apart the worn seams.

At last!

Hands shaking with hunger, with the urgency of need, Malik tugged at the buttons halfway down the prim white blouse, pulling them open roughly. The small opening he made was just enough to let him push his fingers in and touch the warm, swelling softness of one exposed breast. At the feel of his caress Abbie choked some incoherent, wordless sound of response, her eyes closing ecstatically, her mouth blindly seeking his.

Another button popped free from its restraint and now he could get his whole hand underneath her blouse. He cupped the softness of one breast, feeling its heat through the silk and lace confection of her bra. The nub of her nipple pushed into his palm in wanton demand and the ache of desire between his legs was almost unbearable.

He had to have her. Had to…

But, even as he closed his hand around her heated softness, his ears caught the sound outside the room that broke into and shattered the sensual delirium that had him in its possession.

CHAPTER THREE

'I'LL leave that with you then…'

The voice sounded out in the hallway, coming clearly through the barely closed door. Calm and decisive and totally shattering to the heated mood that gripped the pair of them.

'We'll sort it out later.'

A male voice.

James Cavanaugh's voice.

His *host's* voice.

The voice of the man he had come here to negotiate with.

What the hell was he doing?

Dazed, shaken, blinking like a man dealing with the aftermath of a blow to his head, Malik lifted his eyes to lock with Abbie's silver gaze. He found that she too had frozen into immobility, her eyes wide and staring straight at him. She looked glazed, unfocused, not seeing anything, and her head was tilted slightly to one side as if she was straining to hear.

'Cavanaugh…' he managed, his voice croaking roughly. 'My—'

She swallowed hard, unable to continue to form the words. 'Your boss.'

Malik nodded, understanding the embarrassment she would feel at being caught like this—especially with the important visitor that the family must want to impress and please as much as possible.

Your boss?

It took the space of a couple of uneven breaths for the words to penetrate the buzzing haze of shock that filled Abbie's mind, and even when they did finally hit home they made no sense at all.

Your *boss!*

He thought that she worked for…

But then the sound of movement from behind the door, the sound of footsteps in the hallway, froze the thought in her mind, leaving instead room for her to grasp at a realisation that was far more stunning, more shocking.

Her *father* was outside in the hall.

And he was coming back.

Her father was crossing the hall, coming back, heading for the library, coming back to his guest…

He would open the door, would look across the room and he would find…

He would find her *here*, like…

With the instinct of panic her hand went to the gaping front of her blouse, fingers spread wide to cover the exposed white skin, the delicate flesh still slightly reddened by the touch of Malik's hard fingers.

'Here…'

Already Malik was moving, acting—taking charge. Already his behaviour was totally back under control—the control she had completely, abjectly lost without a hope of finding again.

He was tugging down her skirt, smoothing it over her hips, along her thighs, his movements brusque and—that damn word again!—controlled. He didn't seem aware of the way that his touch, so cool and calm, distant as a doctor's, made her want to cry out in shock and loss as it came so close to the spot where the throbbing tension of need even now held her in its grip. The sting of arousal still pricked at her breasts, demanding appeasement. The whole of her body felt like a long moan of protest at the way that the pleasure it had been seeking had been so brutally snatched away, leaving her lost and desolate.

'Fasten yourself up.'

Malik's tone was brusque, his curt words a cold command. His eyes were hard as jet without any trace of the burn of warmth that had been in them before. The man who had called himself 'just Malik' was gone and the person that Abbie thought of as *The Sheikh* was back and wholly in control.

He was busy tidying himself as he spoke, quickly and efficiently fastening the buttons her fingers had tugged open, tucking his shirt back into his trousers, smoothing his hand over his tousled hair.

'I said, fasten yourself up!'

It was an order and a sound of reproof all in one and the cold disapproval in the black gaze that swept over her cut straight to her heart.

She had been lost, adrift on a sea of passion so intense that it had taken over her mind and driven all rational thought from it. The sensation had been so devastating that she was having trouble focusing on anything else. But Malik was icily, unemotionally back in control in the space of a heartbeat, and it was obvious that nothing at all had touched him in the way that it had affected her.

'Do you want Cavanaugh to find you here like this?'

'N-no…'

She could only manage a whisper, her voice refusing to obey her. So were her fingers as she fumbled with her disordered clothing, the sense of panic at the thought of her father finding her like this making matters worse.

'Abbie!'

Her name hissed through Malik's teeth in a sound of total exasperation and he reached for her again. Perhaps his intention was only to help; perhaps he meant to do what she couldn't manage and pull things back together again, but that wasn't the thought that crossed Abbie's mind.

'No!'

Remembering only the burning pleasure that those hands had brought her just seconds before and not knowing whether she most longed for a repetition of it or feared it utterly, she reacted on total instinct. An instinct that was even closer to the panic she had barely been able to control.

'*No*—I—I have to go!'

There was one way she could avoid any confrontation with her father, ensure that he didn't know what had been happening in his absence. There was a side door on the far wall of the library, one that led out of the room in the opposite direction to that in which her father was approaching.

True, it also led to the conservatory from which the only way back into the house, without retracing her steps, was to go out into the garden and come in again by the kitchen door. But at least she would have a few moments in which to draw breath. Everyone was inside so she would have time in which to pull herself together, both mentally and physically.

How could she have let this happen? How could she have lost all control, all sense of self-preservation so completely as to forget just who this man was and why he was here?

She couldn't even look him in the face, couldn't meet his eyes. And yet just seconds ago…

'Your boss,' Malik had said. He had thought that she was employed by her father—by the Cavanaugh family. She could only suppose that the appalling apron and her scruffy clothes had given him that impression.

He thought that she was only a servant and so fair game for him to waste time with, to flirt with heartlessly. To use for his pleasure and then discard when he felt like it.

'I have to go,' she muttered again, hoping it sounded more convincing this time. With her head down, her eyes burning with bitter humiliation, she turned for the door, moving as quickly as she could, just wanting to get away—get out of there.

She made it to the door, had turned the handle—opened it—when, to her shock and horror, he came after her. One strong bronze-skinned hand closed over her arm, imprisoning her wrist, holding her.

'Wait!' he said, his voice low and thick. 'Wait!'

'Wait for what?'

For further humiliation? For him to tell her that she wasn't worth his time? That she had simply been an amusement with which to fill the minutes while he had been waiting for her father to return? Wasn't that what men like him—sheikhs like him—had harems for? So that they could pick any woman they chose. Any woman who happened to catch his eye. Any woman he fancied mauling.

'So that you can maul me again?'

'Maul?'

He actually looked shocked. His proud dark head went back, brilliant eyes narrowing sharply.

'*Maul!*' he repeated on a deeper note. 'You dare to call that mauling! Let me remind you, *sukkar*, that you wanted it every bit as much as I did—you still do.'

His cruel gaze dropped to where her breasts were still exposed. To where the tight, hungry points of her nipples betrayed the need she might try to deny with words—an unconvincing denial when her body spoke so eloquently against her.

'And I still do.'

Malik's voice was rough and thick. So he wasn't quite as much in control as he pretended, Abbie realised. There was still a lingering rawness in his eyes and the hand that imprisoned hers was not quite as steady as she had first thought.

The realisation made her hesitate. She couldn't move, either in or out of the open door. She could only stare up into the glittering darkness of his eyes and wait...

But then the footsteps—her father's footsteps paused outside the door. She saw the handle turn…

And suddenly Malik's hand came up to touch her face. He cupped her cheek in one hard palm, looked deep into her eyes as if determined to hypnotise her into total obedience.

'Come to me tonight,' he whispered softly, huskily. 'Come to me at my hotel and we can finish what we started.'

She didn't answer. She couldn't answer. But she knew from his faint smile how he saw the change in her face, the one she couldn't disguise. The one that meant acquiescence, whether it was wise or not.

He saw her face change and knew he didn't have to say anything more.

'The Europa,' he said, the total confidence in his tone that of a man who knew he had won and there was nothing more to say. 'The Europa at eight. I'll be waiting.'

His mouth took hers for a hot, brief moment and then was gone.

Abbie didn't know if she moved herself or if Malik pushed her, but either way it was only just in time. Somehow she was on the other side of the door, and with it firmly closed behind her. And in the library she heard the other door open and her father's voice apologising for being so long.

'Not at all…'

This time, Malik's accented voice came clearly through the heavy wood that separated them. Cool and clear and totally unperturbed as if nothing had happened and he had simply been standing there, waiting for his host's return.

'I had plenty to think about. Plenty to occupy me while I waited. I never noticed the time at all.'

It was already turning dusk outside. Under cover of the gathering darkness, Abbie swiftly tidied herself up, adjusted her appearance. The wretched apron was ruined, torn beyond repair, so she pulled it off, crumpling it into a bundle and stuffing it out of sight behind a couple of plant pots. She would come back and retrieve it later tonight, when no one was likely to see her.

Later tonight. Tonight. The word hit home to her as she hurried along the shadowy path, heading for the kitchen door.

Tonight. Come to me tonight...and we can finish what we started.

He had been so sure, so confident that she would not refuse him. He would be waiting for her at eight, just as he had said.

Would she be there?

Even as the question entered her head, Abbie knew that the answer would push it straight out again, giving her no time to think. Not that she needed any.

Of course she would be there. She had no other choice. No alternative.

It was dangerous. It was crazy. It was probably the most stupid thing she would ever do—but how could she ever live with herself if she didn't do it? How could she leave this stunning man, this devastating meeting, only half known, his lovemaking only half completed? The ache in her body, an ache that felt like a bruise right into her soul, told her that she couldn't. She just couldn't leave things like this.

The Europa at eight...

Malik's confident voice rang inside her head.

He was so sure that she would be there.

Her footsteps slowed, coming to a halt in the darkness, and her fingers crept up to her mouth, pressing against her lips, thinking back, remembering how it had felt to have Malik's kiss on her mouth. His caresses on her yearning body.

The Europa at eight...

And she would be there. Of course she would be there. How could she ever live with herself if she wasn't?

CHAPTER FOUR

THE huge gilt clock in the foyer of the Europa hotel was striking the half hour as Abbie made her way to the reception desk.

She was exactly half an hour late—deliberately so. She had fully intended that Malik should have to wait for her. Or at least she had once she had finally decided that she was coming here tonight. Because the confidence of that first decision hadn't lasted. She had barely got inside the house, closing the kitchen door and leaning back against it, before the doubts had assailed her.

How could she have ever been so stupid? she had asked herself. What was she thinking of, planning to go to him— to take him up on his invitation?

His invitation to seduction.

No, it hadn't been an invitation. It was an order—a command from a man used to giving commands to everyone every day. Giving them and having people jump to obey them as soon as he spoke. He probably didn't even have to ask most of the time, just click his fingers and he would be obeyed.

And was she going to jump to do his bidding too?

Not on her life!

No, she told herself as she made her way through to the hall again. His Royal High and Mightiness the Arrogant

Sheikh Malik bin Rashid Al'Qaim could snap his fingers all he liked. She wasn't going to be at his beck and call just because...

Just because he was the most devastatingly attractive, the most shockingly sexy man she had ever met in her life.

Her footsteps slowed, turned, drawn by some invisible force, some powerful magnetism, taking her towards the library in spite of the resistance she tried to impose on them. The door was tightly shut, the sounds of the voices inside the room muffled, their words impossible to make out. But she knew when Malik was speaking She had only heard a few hundred words from that erotic voice but already it seemed to be imprinted on her mind so that she recognised it instantly.

And wanted to hear it again.

And again.

She wanted to hear it tell her to call him 'Just Malik'. To hear him say that she was beautiful, that he wanted her... She wanted to hear that glorious voice whisper to her in the darkness, giving her words of love, of caring, of hunger.

Tonight. Come to me tonight...and we can finish what we started.

Oh, dear God, she just wanted to listen to that voice all night—every night—for the rest of her life.

But was that enough to base her future on? Surely she was totally unwise—crazy!—to go to him.

But, oh! How she *wanted* to.

'Can I help you, madam?'

The receptionist's question broke into her thoughts and dragged her back to the present. To the moment she had been worrying about from the point she had set out on this wild assignation.

'Come to me,' Malik had said, and he'd told her the name of the hotel, but he hadn't given her any further information than that. She had never visited someone so important, someone royal before. Surely there would be security checks at the very least.

'My name is Abbie…' she began hesitantly and was intensely relieved to see the woman's face break into a smile.

'Of course. We are expecting you. Would you please come this way?'

A few moments later, whizzing upwards in the express lift that went only to Malik's suite, Abbie couldn't believe how easy it had been. She had merely given her name and everyone had jumped into action, informing the penthouse suite that she was here, checking her identity, escorting her to the lift. There she had been handed over to the care of a tall, dark and deeply polite security guard who now stood, strong legs planted firmly on the floor, deep-set eyes alert and watchful, on the opposite side of the lift.

Just at that moment it slowed to a halt and the doors slid open silently. Her companion gave a small bow.

'After you, madam,' he said as he stood back to allow her to precede him.

This must be what it was like all the time if you were a sheikh, Abbie reflected as she stepped out on to thick, soft pile carpeting in a rich royal blue. To have people whose only job was to follow your instructions, to do as they were told, to do as you asked. Once again Sheikh Malik had snapped his fingers and everyone had jumped to do his bidding.

If she had been nervous before, then now her stomach felt as if a million desperate butterflies were beating frantic wings against her ribcage, sending waves of unease up into her throat. She struggled for breath as she headed into the small foyer where a smooth, pale wooden door barred her way. Another security guard stood beside it, firmly at attention, arms by his sides, the smooth fitting of his tailored jacket very slightly marred by an ominous-looking bulge at his waistband.

Abbie swallowed hard at just the thought of being this

close to a gun, forcing herself to smile nervously into the guard's dark, set face. But her attempt at a polite greeting was ignored as, with another of those small, stiff bows, he reached to open the door and hold it for her.

'Th-thank you!'

Her legs seeming to have only the strength of cotton wool, Abbie stumbled into the room, her personal security guard following close behind her. From behind, she heard the man say something in Arabic, obviously announcing her. As she blinked to clear eyes that had blurred with tension, she saw Malik's tall, elegant figure uncoil smoothly from the soft black leather-covered settee set in the middle of the huge luxurious room.

'You came!' he said, the impact of that rich honeyed voice hitting her senses hard all over again. 'Welcome!'

Had he really questioned that she would appear? Privately, Abbie took the liberty of doubting that he had thought any such thing. Men like Malik never even considered that there was any likelihood that they would not be obeyed, and obeyed without question.

But then she remembered the stunning news that her father had given her over dinner. The news that had totally changed her mind when it had been set against coming here at all.

She had decided that she was going to be sensible. That she couldn't take the risk of doing as Malik had asked, no matter how much her foolish heart had pleaded with her. And then her father had said that he had something to discuss with her.

'It's Andy, isn't it?' she'd said apprehensively, seeing the way his face was set into lines of strain, his blue eyes shadowed with concern.

'The Sheikh has told you something—what has he said? Will they let him go?'

'There is a chance,' James Cavanaugh had responded. 'But it's going to be difficult.'

'However difficult it is, you have to do it!' Abbie had declared. 'You *have* to. You can't leave him there in that jail, locked up for…'

Her words had faltered nervously, dying on her lips as her father shook his head, his expression sombre.

'Why are you looking at me like that?' she'd asked. 'What does he want? What is it you're not saying?'

'It isn't a question of my doing something,' her father had told her solemnly. 'The only person who can help your brother is you. You're the one who has it in your power to help him, but I don't know if you can possibly agree to what's been asked…'

'Come and sit down…'

Malik was moving towards her, his hand outstretched. Without even really knowing that she was doing it, Abbie pushed her own hands into the pockets of the blue-and-white dress she wore, putting them securely out of reach. If he was to touch her, she didn't know what her reaction would be. Just being in the room with him was bad enough.

She had told herself that she hadn't been thinking straight. That she had been so desperately on edge all day—all week!—worrying about her brother, fearful of the moment that the all-powerful sheikh would arrive, dreading the thought of the demands he might make to free Andy. She must have exaggerated the stunning impact this man had had on her.

She had to have exaggerated it. No man could have launched such an assault on her senses, driven her so out of her mind that it had left her shaking with reaction long after she had left him.

But Malik had. And she hadn't overstated a thing! Even now, when he was still several metres away from her, she could feel her senses start to react, like a flower unfurling in the sun, turning towards the heat and the light, drawn irresistibly to what it needed most.

Her heartbeat had already quickened and her pulse was throbbing. The clean masculine scent of his body was in her nostrils, making her quiver in response.

At some point he had changed his clothes and now here, in the privacy of this huge suite, he was surprisingly casually dressed in jeans and a clinging T-shirt, black as his hair and eyes. And seeing him like that seemed to dispel the thought that he was a sheikh, a prince, the ruler of his desert country. Instead he was just a man. A devastatingly attractive man. An incredibly, hotly sexy man.

And a man who had made it plain how much he wanted her.

'Abbie?'

He had reached her side and his hand touching her shoulder to draw her attention startled her into new awareness. The heat of his hand seemed to burn through the material of her dress, scorching the skin beneath so much that she didn't know whether she most wanted to lean into it or pull away sharply.

Hot colour flared in her cheeks and she swallowed hard to relieve the uncomfortable pressure in her throat.

'Thank you…'

There was a sense of release in walking away from him. Release from the heated tension that had tightened every muscle, release from the stinging sensitivity to everything about him. But as soon as she moved she knew that she wanted it back again, longed for him to come close once more.

It wasn't easy; it wasn't comfortable. It didn't feel safe or relaxing. The truth was that it knotted her nerves tight with tension and uncertainty. It made her stomach twist just to think of it—but at the same time it was thrilling and exciting. It was the most wonderful thing that had happened to her. It brought her *alive* in a fizzing, crackling way. So alive that it was as if she had only been sleepwalking through her life before.

And on top of that it made her feel so completely, gloriously feminine. She had never felt so much of a woman as she had in the few short hours she had known this man and he had made his desire for her so obvious.

And more than his desire, if what her father had told her was right.

'Can I get you a drink?'

Malik stood beside her as she sank down into the soft comfort of the leather-covered settee, his height and strength so much more imposing from this lower position.

'Please…'

She had to find some way of speaking in more than mono-syllables! Abbie reproved herself. But simply being in this man's presence seemed to have tied her tongue into knots and scrambled her brain so that she couldn't think straight.

'Wine? Or mineral water—or something stronger?'

'Mineral water, please.'

She would do well to keep a clear head and not muddle her thoughts even further with alcohol.

Or perhaps some alcohol would relax her.

'No—wine, please—red. Anything, really. I don't mind. Whatever you've got will be fine.'

Well, at least she was talking in sentences of a sort, but now there was the risk of her tongue running away with her. Clamping her lips shut, Abbie tried again for control, only to find that any hope of it eluded her as she saw the small, almost unconscious hand gesture that Malik made, the auto-matic inclination of his head towards a dresser on which a selection of bottles and glasses stood.

And the immediate move into action that was the result.

She had barely even noticed the man who had been stand-ing at the far side of the room. He had been so still and silent that he had almost blended in with his surroundings, his navy blue shirt and jacket toning with the dark velvet of the ceiling to floor curtains. But now he moved forward, a result of Malik's brief, almost imperceptible summons.

Silent and smooth, he moved to the tray of drinks, opening bottles and pouring without another word needing to be said, then handing them to his prince with a bow.

This was what it would be like all day every day for Malik, Abbie thought on a wave of shock. This was what he was used to, what was normal to him. He was accustomed to be waited on hand and foot, his slightest whim attended to, almost before he had even realised it.

And this would be her life too if…

No, she couldn't think of that now! It would destroy the little composure she had managed to gather together.

But of course it was totally impossible that she could *not* think of it! It was all that had been spinning round and round in her thoughts ever since the moment that her father had told her the conditions that had been offered to enable Andy's release.

'The Sheikh of Barakhara needs a wife. He has chosen you to be that wife. If you say yes, then he will drop all charges against Andy and free him as soon as it can possibly be managed.'

Her father had believed that she couldn't possibly agree to the demands he was making. He had assumed that she would refuse to have anything to do with the idea. That she would declare she would rather die or face prison herself. But then, of course, her father had no idea that she had ever met the Sheikh—met Malik in person.

And he had definitely no suspicion at all of the effect that Malik had had on her.

Something had happened in the time they had been apart, Malik told himself as he took the two glasses—one of wine and one of water—from Ahmed and carried them over to the coffee table before which Abbie was sitting. She had changed—or at least her mood was very different from the sparky, vibrant young woman he had met earlier that day.

There was a stiffness about the way that she held herself,

a wariness in those enormous eyes and she looked as skittish as one of his thoroughbred Arabian mares, as if she might turn and run from him at the slightest suggestion of anything that might spook her. As he put the glasses down her eyes flicked up to his face, very quickly, and then away again, twice as fast. And her 'Thank you,' was so faint as to be almost inaudible.

Well, he knew how to handle an uncertain woman. He was almost as much of an expert in it as he was in soothing a nervous horse. It needed patience, consideration, but the end result was worth it. He would get what he wanted in the end.

And what he wanted out of Abbie was a long night's pleasure. She was to be his relaxation after a day from hell. From the way that she had responded to him earlier, he had anticipated that it would be a lot easier than it now seemed likely. But he could wait. He had all night.

But first he needed to work on the atmosphere a little— make things easier, more comfortable for both of them.

'Leave us.'

A wave of his hand gestured towards the door, indicating that Ahmed and the security guard should leave. Abbie would relax much more if they were alone. The bodyguard would have to remain at the door but at least they would be spared his inhibiting presence in the room.

'So now,' he said, coming to sit opposite her as the door closed behind the other two men, 'we can be alone together.'

Abbie reached for the water, gulped some of it down, setting the glass back on the table with an unsteady crash.

'He—they—walked backwards,' she managed on a raw shaken note.

'Hmm? Oh, Ahmed and Ishaq?'

The truth was that he had barely noticed the other two men leaving the room. His attention had been solely focused on the woman in the blue-and-white dress. The woman whose blonde hair was too tightly fastened back for his liking. Whose huge grey eyes, fringed with lush thick lashes, still had that startled, apprehensive look about them, like a rabbit caught in car's headlight.

'It is the custom in Barakhara.'

'They always have to do that?'

Malik's only response was a curt nod. His half-brother stuck strictly to the old-fashioned rituals expected of servants and here in England he was acting as Jalil's representative so he was accorded the same deference, no matter that he had dispensed with such nonsense in his own kingdom. But he saw that it must seem stunning and almost shocking to her. Of course, it would be that that had put her on edge.

'Don't worry, I won't expect it of you.'

Now what had he done to bring that expression to her eyes? This time she lifted her gaze to his and studied his face searchingly for a moment. And when she reached for her glass it was the wine she drank. Uncertainty or relaxation? He didn't know but he knew which one suited his purposes best.

He didn't want her to sit perched on the edge of the settee like that, her mouth strictly controlled, her hands fastened around her glass as if she feared she might drop it. What he wanted was the woman he had met that afternoon. The woman who had heated his blood so fast it had felt like an explosion in his head. The woman who had melted into his arms like a candle before the blaze of the fire. The dress she had on might be so much more flattering and feminine than the elderly blouse and skirt uniform—and that ridiculous ugly apron—but just the fact that she was wearing it meant that she was wearing too much.

What he wanted was to skip the formalities and get straight to the intimacy she had all but promised him this afternoon. He wanted her out of that dress and whatever little bits of lace she was wearing underneath it. He wanted her naked and responsive, warm, willing and open to him, lying underneath him either here or in the big luxurious bed in the next room—he didn't care where.

And she wanted the same. She wouldn't be here otherwise. He had asked her to come to him, to finish what they had started, and here she was, ready to do just that. It was too late for second thoughts.

And the first thing that had to happen was that appallingly controlled and unappealing hairstyle had to go.

'But I do want this changed…'

Leaning forward, he put his hands around the back of her head, finding the elastic band that restrained the blonde hair. A couple of swift, efficient tugs soon had it sliding down and off the silken ponytail before he tossed it carelessly on the floor, not looking where it fell.

Instead his attention was fixed on her face. On those widening grey eyes, the way that the soft rose mouth had opened on a gasp of surprise. The wineglass she still held remained frozen, the movement to replace it on the table stilled completely.

'That's better…'

With his fingers he combed through the loosened strands, freeing them even more, ruffling them around her face, over her shoulders. At first he was simply acting to ease away the restriction of the severe style but as soon as he felt the slide of the silky hair against his fingers he lost sight of what his original intention had been.

All he knew was that he wanted to stroke, to smooth, to caress…just to touch. He wanted to tangle his fingers in the silken slide of it, to inhale the scent of some floral shampoo that blended with the warmth of the skin on her scalp to create an aroma so potently intoxicating that it made his senses swim just to breathe.

'Much better,' he said on a very different tone, his voice suddenly deeper, husky and thickened by the need that was already gnawing at him deep inside. '*Much* better.'

Abbie made some faint inarticulate sound that might have been agreement then abandoned it on a faint sigh.

She slicked a soft pink tongue over her upper lip as if to ease some dryness there then froze in shock as she caught him watching the tiny betraying movement.

'Malik…' she managed and her voice sounded so much like his, hoarse and fraying at the edges, that he laughed out loud, the sound catching deep in his throat, emerging more as an uneven sigh than the chuckle he had aimed for.

The caress of his hands moved from her hair to her scalp, shaping the fine bones of her skull against his palms, feeling the warmth of her skin. Twisting his fingers in her hair so that he held her gently prisoner, he drew her face towards his.

'Much, much better.'

Her eyes never blinked, never flickered. Their wide grey gaze remained fixed on his until it blurred as their lips met. The kiss was slow, gentle, lingering. It was a greeting, an exploration, an invitation, and it couldn't have been more different from the fierce, passionate kisses they had shared in the library earlier in the afternoon.

But the fierceness, the passion was still there. Malik could sense it hidden just below the surface of the kiss. He could taste it on her mouth, on the moistness of her tongue as it tangled with his so briefly, then slipped away again. Her head fell back against the support of his hands and at last her eyes closed and he felt the warmth of her sigh on his skin.

Malik lifted a finger and traced it down the side of her face, tracing the shape of her cheek, the line of her jaw

'I'm glad you came,' he muttered, kissing those closed eyelids softly.

They fluttered open again, grey eyes looking straight into his, so close that he could see the soft lilac colour that flecked them here and there, in contrast to the black pupil at their heart.

'Did you doubt that I would?' Abbie asked, knowing the answer even before the question.

One corner of his sexy mouth curled up into a wicked, knowing smile.

'Not for a moment,' he told her huskily.

Of course not. Of course he hadn't doubted for a moment that his command that she come here tonight would be obeyed. That she would do exactly as he said. That he had only to crook his little finger and she would jump to obey him, just as his servants had when he snapped his fingers to order drinks or waved a hand to dismiss them.

He'd expected instant obedience and got it from them.

And from her?

Suddenly Abbie needed the fortifying effect of the wine and, tilting her glass, she swallowed down a gulp of the rich ruby liquid. Its warmth flooded her veins, potent and intoxicating, but no more effective than the scent of Malik's skin, the heat of his hand on her face.

'You knew I'd come?'

'I knew you'd come.'

'You're very sure of yourself!'

Malik shook his dark head slowly, denying her accusation.

'I was very sure of you.'

That wandering finger had moved down from her face. Now it was trailing a path under her ear, along the side of her neck, down to her shoulder. Slowly, lazily, Malik hooked it into the loose neckline of her dress and pulled the silky material back, exposing the soft skin.

Just for a moment, he let his strong, tanned fingers rest against the spot where her pulse beat under the skin, the intensity of his glittering black eyes belying the relaxed ease of his movements.

For a couple of seconds he concentrated on the beat of her blood just underneath his fingertips and the knowing, arrogant smile grew by several degrees.

'I knew you wanted me just as much as I wanted you...'

'I…' Abbie began but he leaned even further forward and laid a long finger over her mouth to silence her.

'No protests—no pretence,' he told her softly. 'We both know how it is between us. That's why I knew you would come.'

Glancing down at the wineglass she still held, he reached for it, taking it from her unsure, nerveless fingers and lifting it slightly as if making a toast; he deliberately turned it so that the exact spot where she had drunk from was facing him. Placing his mouth over it he drank from the glass too, the gesture seeming like a pledge of feeling, of togetherness…

…and commitment?

Just for a second her father's unbelievable words floated into her head.

The Sheikh of Barakhara needs a wife. He has chosen you to be that wife.

Yes, she was here because of the way she had felt, the way she had responded to Malik earlier that afternoon. She had always known, even when she'd protested that she would not, that she *would* come to him. She *had* to. But what about that stunning proposal of marriage? Why had Malik not said anything about it? When would he tell her…?

Abbie's thoughts went back to the moment when her father had told her that the price of her brother's freedom was that she should become the Sheikh's bride. She knew he had been stunned when she had actually considered the ultimatum. He had been amazed that she hadn't turned it down flat.

But then he didn't know where she had been planning to go tonight, and who would be waiting for her when she got there. He didn't know that she was already Malik's, heart and soul, and had been from the moment he had first kissed her.

He was right, she admitted to herself. Of course he was right. She would be here anyway, there was no way on earth she could have stayed away.

She would be here, had to be here without any thought of

commitment or a future with him. She just had to know Malik, be with Malik, *love* Malik for as long as he gave her.

So it had seemed impossible, a dream come true, to know that he wanted her so much that he had actually told her father he wanted to marry her.

Okay, so he had muddied the issue by making marriage to him the condition he placed on Andy's release, rather than making any emotional statement, but she thought she understood that. If she felt confused and shaken by the speed and force of her own feelings for him, then how much more so would a man like Malik—coming from a country where men didn't show their feelings openly—and as the ruler of it, no less—hesitate to express his feelings openly? He wanted her and for now that was enough. He wanted her enough to marry her—what more could she ask? It was too early to talk of love, at least for Malik. But when they were together then surely that love would come.

But then Malik moved to sit down beside her on the big black leather settee. His arms came round her tightly and his mouth took hers in a long, sensuous kiss that had her senses swooning in a second.

She dropped her head back against his chest, feeling its strength support her, hearing the heavy pounding of his heart beneath her ear. His scent was all around her, swamping her, invading her. Breathing it in was like inhaling some powerful drug, one that drove all thought from her head and left her intoxicated with need, delirious with hunger. The hunger that this man had woken with his touch on her skin as he had crushed her against the wall in the library that afternoon.

She had fallen into his arms without thinking then, and she fell into them again without a second's hesitation now. Her own arms went up around his neck, her fingers lacing frantically in his hair, clutching at the crisp black strands, pulling his head down so that his lips crushed hers even harder than before. Her mouth opened under his, her tongue teasing, provoking, inviting the intimate invasion that echoed the deeper, more primitive union her body screamed for.

She wanted to hold him there, like that for ever, never letting go, but at last Malik had to lift his head, wrench his mouth away from hers, if only to drag in a raw, much needed, uneven breath.

'So now…' he muttered roughly against her lips, his voice heavy and thick with the same powerful hunger that poured through her veins, pounded at her thoughts. 'I think we should continue from where we had to leave off this afternoon.'

CHAPTER FIVE

IT WAS happening all over again, Abbie sighed inwardly as she surrendered to the sensual power of that kiss, going limp in Malik's arms and giving herself up wholeheartedly to the caress.

She had no hope of wondering, of questioning, of even thinking, when her senses were being besieged in this way. And the truth was that she didn't *want* to think or ask any questions; she just wanted to feel, to melt into the heat of the sensations that were flooding through her and give herself up to them, totally and completely.

Malik held her tight, pulling her up against him as he lay back on the soft cushions, stretching out long legs along the length of the settee. Abbie had just time to feel the heat of him and the force of the thick ridge of his erection against her back before he twisted her around, rolling her over until she lay at his side, her head pillowed on his arm, her body half imprisoned by his.

His hands were in her hair again, tilting her head and positioning it just so that he could reach it with ease, exert the most sexual mastery over her mouth, torment her already fizzing nerves with yet more excitement.

At the same time his hands were exploring her hungry body. They traced out every line of muscle, every curve of flesh, making her shiver in involuntary response under his heated caress.

And when those hard, hot fingers spread over her breast, stroking along one side, cupping the swollen shape through the linen of her dress, she couldn't hold back the low whimper of response that broke from her throat, feeling Malik's sexy mouth curl into a smile against her own.

'You like that?' he murmured, his accented voice rich and warm as a tiger's purr, the pressure of his hand increasing, moulding, shaping her so that she moaned in delight.

'And you'll like this too…'

The feel of the caress changed, lightening, trailing tormenting fingers over her sensitised skin, moving up to where the tight bud of her aroused nipple pushed at the restriction of her clothes, seeking his touch. She heard Malik's laughter deep down in his throat as she felt the response she couldn't hide and he closed his fingers around the pouting nub, tugging, teasing, playing with it until she writhed against him.

'And this…'

Pushing her on to her back, he bent his head, nuzzling at her breast. His mouth closed over the distended nipple, his tongue moistening the fine material until she felt its dampness against her skin. And then, seeming to judge the perfect moment with a faultless instinct, he suckled hard, the combination of heat and moisture, the abrasiveness of her clothing against her sensitised skin making her cry aloud, her head falling back, her eyes closing.

'More… Malik—more!'

It was choked from her, impossible to hold back. All her inhibitions seemed to have burned up in the blazing flames inside her head, melting in the boiling heat that seared her blood. And once more she felt the warm breath that his laughter pushed against the skin at the neckline of her dress.

'Oh, I have a lot more in mind,' he promised darkly. 'But I think we would be much more comfortable in my bed…'

With her eyes closed, she felt him swing his legs to the floor, gathering her into his arms and getting to his feet in one smooth movement. Instinctively she flung her arms around his neck, burying her face against the bronzed column of his throat, suddenly afraid that even a glimpse of reality in the form of the room they were crossing might bring her out of the heated dream in which she was lost.

And wanted to stay lost.

Some sort of strange, exotic magic seemed to have taken over her world from the moment Malik had appeared in it. One moment she had been ordinary—lonely and afraid for her brother trapped in a prison far away. The next, this amazing, stunning man had swept into her life, literally sweeping her off her feet.

Men like Malik, men who had the power of imprisonment, of freedom, over her brother, didn't want girls like her. He could have his pick of any one of a thousand society beauties, beauties from every country in the world, so why should he even look twice at her?

But he had. He'd not only looked, he'd liked what he'd seen. More than liked—he wanted her. More than wanted. He had told her father that he wanted to marry her…

And that thought was too much to take in. Too much to believe. It made her draw in her breath so sharply, so deeply that the scent of Malik's skin overwhelmed her again, making her head spin.

Still with her eyes closed, she let her face press closer to the source of the musky erotic perfume, pressed her lips against the side of his neck where his pulse throbbed underneath her mouth. She let her tongue slide out to taste the faintly salty tang of his skin and felt his heartbeat kick up a pace. He muttered something thick and rough in his native language and, quickening his pace, crossed the lounge in several long, fierce strides. The bedroom beyond took even less time and then she was tumbled on to the crisp white cotton of the bed, almost buried in the softness of the duvet, crushed even further by the weight of Malik's body as he came down beside her.

'Beautiful, beautiful Abbie...'

Her name was a soft crooning sound as he spread her out on the bed, kissing her face, her still-closed eyelids, her hair. Once more, that tormenting mouth pressed against her own but when she would have responded, lifting her head from the pillows to kiss him back, he was already gone, moving over her body, unable to stay still, kissing every spot her could find, making her nerves sing in yearning response.

Those wicked hands were busy with the fastening of her dress, finding the long zip at the back and easing down, pulling the soft material away from her body and pressing yet more kisses on the exposed flesh revealed to him. Her bra was dealt with in the same speedy, efficient way, no uncomfortable or embarrassing fumbling dragging her from the burning golden haze that made her whole body glow in hot excitement.

The heat seemed to have pooled between her legs so that even the finest soft tights she wore seemed desperately restricting, the delicate, barely-there silk of her underwear clinging and tight. She moved restlessly, urgently, tossing her head on the pillows, burying her heated cheeks in the cool of the covers.

'Easy, *sukkar*, easy,' Malik soothed, stroking a calming hand over her burning face and taking her mouth again in a slow, drugging kiss. 'Let's not rush things—not this first time.'

'No...' Abbie didn't know how she managed to form the word. When she let it out in a long moaning sigh she had no idea at all whether she was agreeing with him that they should take their time or trying to voice a protest at the delay in the appeasement of the hungry demands of her body.

Malik was kissing his way down the length of her now, making her writhe with delight as his hot mouth moved over the soft flesh he had exposed. His kisses marked out a burning path along her shoulders, down her ribcage and under the swell of her breasts. She wished he would take the aching tip of one of them in that sensual mouth, but instead he continued on his way down over the softness of her belly, teasing her navel with a wicked slide of his tongue.

'Malik…' she sighed, reaching down restless hands to close over his shoulders, wanting to drag him up to her hungry mouth again.

But her mood changed very slightly as her fingers tangled in the black cotton of his T-shirt, reminding her that, although she was almost naked, he was still fully dressed.

'You're wearing too many clothes.' She pouted.

'I agree.' Malik's response was muffled against her skin. 'But it's a matter that's easily remedied.'

He proved his point by tugging off the T-shirt so quickly that Abbie barely noticed his lips had left her body before they were back again, kissing her so seductively that her toes curled, her lower body twisting up against his. The potent force of his arousal rubbed against her pelvis, making her burn hotter and hungrier than ever before.

'And *you* have more on than I like,' Malik muttered roughly.

He hooked his thumbs in her remaining flimsy garments and wrenched them down along her thighs. His movements were so forceful that Abbie heard the fine tights rip and hole, her knickers not faring any better. But she didn't care and a moment later she was incapable of considering *anything* when Malik's mouth kissed its way through the light curls at the top of her legs, his tongue seeking the tight bud of her clitoris and teasing it into yearning life.

His breath was hot against the soft folds of her sex, adding an extra dimension to the need that made her toss restlessly against the pillow. She wanted him to go on—and on—but at the same time she needed so much more. She needed the reality of his possession, the sense of his heat and hardness filling her, taking her…

'M-Malik…'

This time her hands tangled in his hair, tugging softly, trying to bring his handsome head and that tormenting mouth towards her. Her mouth needed his; her breasts burned for the touch of his tongue, the tug of his mouth. And deep inside her she wanted that most forcefully male part of him, the hunger the most fiercely primitive she had ever known.

At first he resisted her, using his tongue to torment her still further, both adding to the delight he had been creating and yet making her so hungry for more that the pleasure was as cruel as a pain.

'Malik!' she protested, fingers twisting the black strands, pulling harder. This time he let himself be moved, giving in to her urging and sliding back over her body, but deliberately taking his time, delivering yet more kisses to her already burning skin.

'What is it you want, *habibti*?'

She could feel the smile on his mouth against her zinging nerves.

'Is it this…?'

His mouth caressed the curve of her right breast, making her cry aloud in fierce delight.

'Or this…?'

This time he sealed her lips with his own, catching the moaning cry in his own mouth and swallowing it down as his tongue tangled with hers, his hands pushed into her hair at the side of her head, holding her face so that she couldn't move away from him.

'Or perhaps what you want is this…'

She was still tasting him on her tongue, on her lips, but already he had slipped away, his mouth taking one breast so suddenly, so fiercely that she screamed aloud with the stinging torment of delight he inflicted on her, hot tears of joy springing to her eyes, spilling out on to her cheeks.

'Yes…yes…yes…'

It was a chant of wildly erotic delight, her voice soaring

up into a near shout of ecstasy, then fading back again to a whimper of pure pleasure as that tormenting mouth first suckled hard and then softly soothed the stinging nipple with his tongue.

'Oh, yes—' she sighed '—oh yes…'

But, wonderful as it was, it still wasn't quite enough. Each movement of his long, hard body on hers reminded her that, while she might be naked, Malik still wore his jeans, the rough denim abrading her skin and coming as a barrier between the throbbing heat at the centre of her and the fierce pulse of his erection.

And she wanted to know the full force of that demand. To feel it probe the female core of her body, to know the swollen fullness deep inside her.

'Malik—I want you—need you…'

'Soon, *sukkar*, soon,' Malik crooned against her breasts, punctuating the words with devastating little slicks of his tongue over her swollen and hot nipple. 'You must learn patience—to wait…'

'I don't want to wait! I want you now!'

'But I told you, we have all the time we need. We have all night.'

All night. It had a wonderful, wonderful sound. So wonderful that she couldn't hold back the swift, flashing smile of pure delight, pure happiness.

All night—tonight. And then…

'All night and every other night.' Abbie sighed. 'Every night of our married lives.'

'*What?*'

If the silence after that one single explosive word was devastating, then his sudden appalling stillness was even worse. It seemed as if Malik had frozen completely, every limb taut and stiff with rejection, every kiss and caress ceasing in a second.

With the moisture from his tongue drying, cooling, stinging on her aroused nipple, the thunder of need pounding at her nerves, throbbing in her body, sending a hungry pulse into her brain, Abbie felt as if she had suddenly dropped from a great height and was falling, falling, spinning and tumbling sickeningly. She was blinded by shock, deaf and breathless with it too. Every word she might have managed was snatched away from her, broken off in her throat, impossible to find in the devastation that was her thoughts. She had fallen out of the world she knew, out of the warmth and sensual delight of the bedroom, out of the comfort of the bed and Malik's lovemaking. Had fallen into a cold, dark, bleak alien world in which nothing fitted any more, nothing made sense and she had no idea where or even quite who she was and what had happened to shatter the existence she had once known.

'What did you say?'

If the first sense of shock at what Abbie had said had hit Malik like a toss of cold water in his face, freezing him in confusion, then the second, full realisation of just what she'd meant went through him like a burning electrical shock. It rocked his sense of reality and made him reel back in an explosive combination of disbelief and horror at what might be involved.

Every night of our married lives.

Had he really been so damn stupid that he hadn't seen what was coming? Had he let his desire for this woman trick him into an area where he was usually much too wily and aware to be caught? Had he in fact not spotted a honey trap when it was baited with such luscious sensuality and had only woken up to find that a spider had him in its sticky imprisoning web when it was almost too late?

A beautiful, sexy, shockingly appealing spider, it was true, but a spider nevertheless. A spider who now stared up at him with wide dazed-looking grey eyes, her soft pink lips, still swollen from his ardent kisses, slightly apart in shock at his reaction.

'I...' she began but the sound of her voice was enough to

jolt him out of the stillness into which he had frozen. His long body jacknifing away from her, he flung himself off the bed and partly across the room.

Only then did he feel he had himself under control enough to turn back and confront her.

'*What* did you say?' he demanded, the brutal control he was having to impose on his feelings, the hard, hungry—*hurting*—protests that his awakened senses were making at the vicious way he had stamped on the pleasure they had anticipated, making his voice harsher than even he had ever heard it before.

Cold-eyed, he watched her wince, flinch back against the pillows, but he squashed down the flicker of remorse that struggled against his anger. He had said nothing about marriage, had promised her nothing. Visions of the possible repercussions if she let her story out flashed into his head. The tabloid press would have a field day. He could see the headlines now—

Sexy Sheikh bedded me then betrayed me.

He promised me marriage but left me wandering in a loveless desert.

'Tell me!' he roared, using the black fury to drive away the temptation to let himself be distracted by the sight of her. She lay there, still spread-eagled on the bed, her delicious body openly displayed, pink-tipped breasts tilted towards him, seeming still to demand—to plead for—his attention.

Damn her! She looked so appealing—so damnably tempting and it was all that he could do not to go straight back to her and finish what he'd started.

It was what his body wanted to do. His heart was thudding, making his blood pound inside his head, and his hotly swollen penis throbbed with hunger and the cruel frustration it was enduring. It was impossible to think straight—and yet he had to if he was to salvage something from this appalling mess—and fast!

'Tell me…' This time he injected his words with a deadly poison and at last that seemed to get through to her. She stirred faintly, blinked her eyes, licked her lips.

Lips that still bore the imprint of his kisses, that must taste of his mouth when she slicked her tongue over them. He could still taste *her* on his own mouth, the lingering flavour of her tongue making desire kick him hard where he already ached with it, making his anger twist a notch higher as a result.

'Our—our married life,' she stammered. 'The life we'll have together when we—we're married…'

So he hadn't been hearing things. He hadn't let passion drive him so completely out of his mind that he hadn't caught what she was actually saying and instead had misinterpreted it, putting in its place something so wild and crazy that it could only be the result of the heat of his blood making his brain cells fuse in need and invent something that was the result of his wild imagination.

'"Our married life",' he repeated, lacing each word with the darkest, most savage sarcasm he could find. No woman had ever heard that tone from him before—and no man in Edhan could have borne it without flinching, trembling at the thought that he had angered his ruler so badly. 'I don't remember offering you marriage. In fact, I don't recall the word ever even being used. So will you kindly tell me just what put the thought into your mind?'

CHAPTER SIX

'WHAT put…'

She was a great little actress, he would give her that. She actually looked as if he had slapped her in the face, opening and closing her mouth as if in shock.

Shock that her little trick hadn't worked, more likely. That her scam to blackmail him—to get as much out of him as she could—had failed.

That had to be the reason for it, surely. She couldn't possibly ever have imagined that he was really going to *marry* her.

'What…' Abbie tried again and the pretence at being stunned, the way she was clearly trying to play on his sensibilities, on his conscience, only infuriated him further. Where gold-diggers were concerned he had no conscience, none at all.

'In your own time,' he snarled, tossing the sarcasm at her like a blow.

'I'd answer if you let me get a word in!'

Oh, now she was showing her true colours! The change of mood revealed what the sweet, innocent female act had hidden all the time. And behind the mask was a snapping vixen. A beautiful little bright-eyed, neat-featured female fox, but one whose sharp white teeth could administer a deadly wound if he let her.

She was a fool to let the mask slip this easily. He was fore-warned and would be much more on his guard than before.

Privately Malik cursed himself for not being fully on his guard from the start. He should have known that his wealth and position would always make him a potential target for the gold-diggers of this world, but, damn it, he had been so attracted to Abbie from the start that stupidly all such thoughts had gone out of the window.

Of course, he'd forgotten the attack she had launched at him in the first moments of their meeting, when they had been alone in the library at the Cavanaughs' house. He should have taken that as a warning. She had been determined to accuse him of cruelty, of ill-treating her precious Andy, and all he'd been able to think about was how beautiful she was, how sexy, how infinitely desirable.

He couldn't believe how damn stupid he had been. He had let basic lust, his body's most primitive needs blind him to what was really happening. How the hell had he let her get past his guard like that? He had enough experience not to take risks. He would have sworn he was not so easily conned.

But she had managed to deceive him well and truly and now all he could do was to practise careful damage limitation to make sure that matters went no further.

'Then speak!' he flung at her.

But it seemed that that only incensed her further.

'Don't take that tone with me, *Your Highness!*'

The spin she put on the title turned it into something that was light years away from the respect he was used to. No woman had ever spoken to him in that way in his life. And no woman had ever pulled herself up on the bed where he had left her and spat fury into his face as she was doing. Every woman he had taken to bed had shown him a proper respect and they had known that marriage was the last thing on his mind. When he married he would not just be looking for a wife, but also for a queen.

'I'm trying to answer if you would only let me!'

'Be my guest…'

He accompanied the words with a mocking little bow.

One that Abbie felt like a cold-blooded slap in the face. She wished so much that she'd not let him pressure her into snapping. She could have bitten her tongue as soon as the words were out. But she hadn't been able to think straight as it was. Malik's reaction had rocked her sense of reality, leaving her thoughts spinning sickeningly. He'd behaved as if she had suddenly turned into a hissing, spitting snake, and then he'd bombarded her with demands, flinging the hard words into her face before she'd had a chance to draw breath and try to think.

So had her father got it all totally wrong? Had he made an appalling error and misheard—misinterpreted—what Malik had said? But he had been so sure! So definite!

The Sheikh of Barakhara needs a wife. He has chosen you to be that wife.

What was there to mistake about that?

But perhaps he'd wanted to tell her about it himself—to propose in his own time and his own way. After all he was a sheikh—a ruler—a king. He wouldn't be at all pleased to find that someone had pre-empted him and revealed his wishes before he was ready.

Or perhaps he'd rethought the whole idea? Had had second thoughts about everything? Had finally decided not to demand marriage? Oh, dear God, had he decided not to show mercy to Andy at all?

Oh, she'd been *stupid* to reveal the fact that she knew about his plans, foolish to have let the heat of passion push the declaration from her lips at just the wrong moment. But she hadn't expected the ferocity of his reaction, the sheer black fury in which he'd rounded on her as if she had suggested that he sell his soul to the devil—or worse.

In the end she'd reacted in pure self-defence. Though

she'd known the hot words were a mistake as soon as she'd said them.

'At least let me put some clothes on first!'

She felt so dreadfully exposed like this, naked in front of those pitch-black, accusing eyes, that furious glare.

'Why?' Malik tossed back at her. 'I'm enjoying the view.'

'I'm sure you are, but I don't intend to provide a strip show for you!'

'You were happy enough to do so a moment or two ago.'

'But that was…'

She couldn't find the strength to finish her sentence, her voice dying away to a whisper as she met the full blaze of his furious glare. Standing there so tall and proud, handsome head flung back, looking down his long aquiline nose at her, he was pure arrogant Arab chieftain from head to toe. And he didn't have to worry about the embarrassment of being suddenly abandoned without a stitch to cover him. He still had his jeans on, the waistband and the zip unfastened as a result of her urgent, seeking hands, making her face heat fierily to remember. The wide expanse of his chest, the bronze skin lightly hazed with black hair, only added to the wild, primitive impression, making him look too untamed, too elemental to belong in the luxurious surroundings of the hotel suite.

'That was when…'

Abbie couldn't help recalling how, when she had first seen him, she had been stunned by how sleek and sophisticated he had looked. How urbane and—and civilised.

Civilised! She almost laughed out loud at the irony of the thought but the sudden fear that he would take it completely the wrong way had her clamping her mouth shut on the revealing reaction. Which only made matters so much worse by turning it into a sort of a weak, smothered whimper.

'That was when what?' Malik prompted harshly, what little patience he had exhausted by even the brief time it took her to struggle to squash down the unwanted nervous laughter.

'When you thought that I wanted to marry you? That I would pay for my pleasure with a circle of gold that bound you to me for life? Was that what made your *strip show* respectable? What justified you coming to my bed without a second's hesitation?'

'No…'

She was starting to shiver inside, as much from the effect of his cold, cutting words as from the fact that she was stark naked sitting on his bed.

But the truth was that her skin was warm, both the central heating in the room and the rush of mortified blood through her veins making her burn in desperate humiliation. It was the way that Malik had changed. The way that the ardent, passionate lover had suddenly become this brutal-toned, set-faced monster whose icy words lashed at her exposed flesh like a whip, making her insides quiver in apprehension and her nerves twist into tight painful knots.

'Because I don't recall you holding out for a ring on your finger then.'

'No…'

It was all that Abbie could manage. All that she could force past her trembling lips.

What was the point in trying to deny it? She *couldn't* deny it! She had been his for the taking from that first kiss, that first touch—from before then. Perhaps she had been his from the first moment she had seen him. From the second that he had turned those fierce black eyes on her as she'd stood in the window watching his arrival.

He had looked at her and she had become his just as surely as if the brilliant black gaze had been like a fiery brand of old. Marking her out as his—his servant—his *slave* to do with as he pleased.

So she had come here tonight knowing she had no option, no other choice. She was his and there was no way she could deny it.

'*Come to me tonight,*' he had said, '*...and we can finish what we started.*'

And she had obeyed his command.

But because of what her father had told her, she had come here tonight with a whole new sense of excitement and happiness. She would never have dared to allow herself to hope—to dream that Malik might care for her, that he might do more than just want her. She had been prepared to settle for that. So when she had been informed that he wanted to marry her, she had been fizzing with delight and excitement, unable to believe that this might be possible.

She had fallen into Malik's arms—into his bed—without a heartbeat of hesitation. This was the man she wanted and he wanted her—for a lifetime, it seemed.

So how had it all turned so sour? How had her father got it so terribly, terribly wrong?

'No...' She sighed again.

'No,' Malik echoed in cruel satisfaction. 'No—because then you were too hot for me—too damn lustful to care. So tell me, *habibti*, just when did this wild idea that I wanted to marry you slip into your pretty head? When you saw the suite—the number of my attendants? Or did you have the whole idea planned in your scheming mind from the start?'

'Planned?'

Abbie wished she could think more clearly, manage to say something—*anything*—other than just stupidly parroting his words back at him.

How could she have planned anything when it was he...?

'Did you come here tonight to get into my bed for two reasons? For your own obvious enjoyment—and then the idea of making a fine profit from it either by blackmailing me into marrying you or...'

'No!'

Abbie had had enough. She still didn't know just what had happened. She had no idea how the terrible mistake had been made—who it had come from. She only knew that her weak, foolish dreams, dreams that had really only just begun to form, had been totally ruined and thrown back in her face by Malik, so that they now lay around her in splinters, shattered beyond repair.

'No, there was nothing like that in my head at all!'

The much needed protection of her clothes was too far away to reach. Even to get hold of her dress would mean going almost to Malik's feet—Malik's still booted feet! she noted on a shudder of reaction—and stooping to snatch up the discarded item from the navy-blue carpet. And that would put her almost in the position of *bowing* and scraping to the horrible man. Which was something she had no intention of doing—ever!

But there was one of those heavy towelling robes that hotels provided for their first class visitors lying on the chair under the window.

'How could I even have thought of that?'

Forcing herself from the bed, she grabbed at the white robe, hauling it up against her, unable yet to face the struggle to find the sleeves, push her arms into them. But at least it served as some sort of protective shield from the fiercely accusing black eyes that seared over her trembling form.

'How could you?' Malik echoed, cold as a hissing snake. 'Oh, somehow I suspect that it was all too easy! You made it plain from the start that you thought I was the evil villain for the way that *Andy* is being treated. What more simple idea than to further your sweetheart's cause by seducing me and blackmailing me afterwards?'

'I did not *blackmail* you.'

There was something very wrong with what Malik had said—some word, some phrases that grated against her desperately raw nerves, telling her that this was why he had got hold of completely the wrong end of the stick. But her thoughts were still buzzing too frantically to let her get a grip on just what it was.

'But only because you didn't get the chance.'

Malik turned unexpectedly and strolled over to the window, where he stood for a few moments staring down at the illuminated city below. Grateful for the brief reprieve, Abbie snatched at the opportunity to pull on the towelling robe. Her hands shook as she pushed them into the sleeves, nerveless fingers fumbling clumsily with the tie belt, but at least it was on and she was covered...

The sudden appalling realisation that Malik had obviously been wearing the robe before her and that it still bore the scent of his skin made her close her eyes on a shudder of purely physical reaction. It was only a few minutes since she had inhaled that musky, intensely personal scent as she lay underneath him, there, on that bed, with her body responding to his, opening to him, just as she had opened her heart...

Immediately she forced her eyes open again. She couldn't let such thoughts into her mind. They would weaken her still more—destroy her if she let them.

As she shifted uneasily on the carpet she felt something soft and light tangle itself around her right ankle and, glancing down, saw to her horror that the lavender-coloured knickers that Malik had pulled down her thighs only moments before were still coiled round one slender ankle. In a flurry of hot embarrassment she kicked herself free, sending the flimsy garment spinning away from her.

'You didn't blackmail me because you didn't play your cards right.'

Malik had turned away from the window and was leaning back against the sill, lean hips propped on the white-painted wood. And once more those burning black eyes were fixed on her pale face in a way that made her tug the robe closer around her, tightening the belt around her waist as much as she could.

'You opened your mouth before you had enough evidence to use against me. What is that saying about putting your foot where your mouth is?'

'Foot *in* your mouth!' Abbie snapped automatically, feeling that little bit safer and more confident with the thickness of the white towelling between her and the glittering glare of those fierce black eyes. 'And why should I want any evidence to use against you?'

'To uphold your crazy story—your fantasy—your lies!'

'My *lies!*'

Abbie's fury almost choked her, making her voice crack on the exclamation.

'I'm no liar!'

'No?'

Malik's stunning face was a mask of contempt as his cold hard gaze seared over her from the top of her head to where her toes curled into the softness of the carpet.

'Then where the hell did you get the idea that marriage was on the cards?'

'Where do you think? My father told me!'

She flung the words at him, wanting to discomfit him, wishing they were actual hard slaps on that handsome, sneering face.

'Your father told you what?'

To her horror Malik didn't appear in the last bit discomfited. If anything, his expression was colder and harder than ever.

'What do you think—Your *Highness*? Isn't it obvious? He told me that you wanted to marry me.'

'He did what?'

Malik's dark head went back, his eyes narrowing until they were just slits above his high, carved cheekbones.

'Then your father is the liar because I said no such thing.'

CHAPTER SEVEN

HER father had told her that he had proposed marriage?

Malik couldn't believe what he was hearing. He wanted to shake his head, slam his hand against the hardness of the window sill, anything to bring himself out of the delusion into which he seemed to have fallen.

Was the woman mad? Or was he dreaming? What sort of a nightmare had he tumbled into without knowing how?

'My father is no liar!'

Did she know what it did to him when she stood up so tall and straight? When she flung back her head and lifted that small stubborn chin so high and proud, silver eyes blazing into his? Did she know how the defiance in her gaze went straight to his groin like a bolt of white-hot lightning, threatening to destroy his ability to think straight—to think at all?

His body still burned with the thwarted passion that had seared through him, melting his bones in its scorching pulse. He didn't dare to fasten the zip of his jeans over the still swollen throb of his sex because just the brush of the loosened material was an agony he could barely endure. And even now the most primitive urgings of his senses were fighting against the cooler warnings of rational thought, demanding that he give in to the needs of his body and fling caution to the winds.

What he wanted most in all the world was to grab this

Abbie, snatch her off her soft little feet and fling her on the bed in front of him. He wanted to rip the stupid oversize robe from her sexy body, strip her naked in seconds and feast his mouth on the satin softness of her skin, know again the taste of her on his lips. He longed to pull her underneath him, bury his hungry body in the welcoming warmth of hers. And she *would* welcome him; he knew that without any doubt.

The blazing fire they had lit between them, the storm of need, could not just be doused in a second, stilled in the space of a heartbeat. His whole body still throbbed with the yearning for fulfilment that had gripped him and hers must feel the same. She must know the nag of frustration, the ache of emptiness that had tortured him ever since the moment he had flung himself from her—know it and want to end it, just as he did now.

If only cold reason didn't warn him of the dangers of taking that sensual path.

Crushing down the erotic thoughts that plagued him, Malik forced himself to face Abbie, to look into her eyes and see not the flashing sexual invitation that she had been offering him just minutes before, but to find instead the cold defiance, the deliberate provocation, the calculated scheming that had brought her here tonight. She had come here to ruin his reputation, to blackmail him for everything she could get and he was not going to let her get away without being punished for that.

'I tell you that your father lied. Or worse. In fact, he made the whole story up. You probably hatched the whole thing between you.'

Once more those eyes flashed, but this time in total rejection of everything he'd said, and she tossed her blonde head in wild defiance.

'I—we did no such thing! There is no plot—no story. Nothing! My father said...'

'"My father said..."' Malik echoed, the burn of dark cynicism in his words. 'Forget it, *sukkar*, drop your lying story now—it will go better for you in the end. Your father can't have spoken of any such thing because the truth of the matter is that I don't know the man—have never spoken to him.'

He'd caught her on the raw there all right, shocking her into silence with the cold dismissal of her lying tale. Her silver gaze lost its sharpness, looked dazed and unfocused. Her soft mouth opened, once, twice, tried to form a retort and failed, closing again slowly as if in despair.

Ruthlessly he pressed home his advantage, hammering home the final nail in the coffin of her lying fiction.

'How could I when your father and I have never met?'

But this time her reaction was the exact opposite of what he had anticipated. Instead of going down under the final blow—giving in and admitting defeat—it was as if something he'd said had stirred her senses again, renewing her conviction, giving her new strength.

The look she turned on him was blazing ice, searing him from head to foot with calculated disdain and cold derision.

'Oh, come on, Your Magnificence!' she scorned contemptuously. 'You are going to have to do better than that! For a moment there you had me worried, but now… Now you might as well give in and admit that *you're* the one who's been trying to lie his way out of this—and not succeeding. You see I *know* you're not telling me the truth now.'

'You know?' Malik questioned, cold and hard as a blade. 'And how…?'

'I'll tell you how.' This time her anger swept her voice right across his coldly phrased question, cutting him off completely. 'I'll tell you how I know. You can't have forgotten that I saw you there—you can't deny that I saw you in the house—in the library.'

'Of course you did.'

Malik's angry gesture dismissed her words, brushing them aside with an impatient flick of his wrist.

'Of course you saw me there. Just as I saw you. It was where we met. Why should I want to deny that I was there? I was waiting for—'

'Waiting for my father,' Abbie put in sharply, harshly, her voice breaking rawly on the last word.

'What did you say?'

Malik's eyes narrowed sharply, a dangerous frown drawing his black brows together.

'Where you were waiting for my father.'

This time the words had a whole new strength about them. A strength that gave them a power of conviction that stopped him dead. Made his head reel.

'When I met you in the library, then you were there because you had come to meet my father. He took you into the library and then later went to speak on the telephone. That's when I came into the room. When I met…'

'When you met me.'

If Malik's thoughts were reeling before, now his head felt as if it was about to explode.

'In the library, I was waiting for James Cavanaugh…'

He caught the slight movement of her head in a faint nod, met the silent accusation of those eyes.

'Damnation, woman—just who is your father? And who the hell are you?'

It couldn't be the way he suspected—could it? Fate couldn't be so malign.

'My name is Abbie Cavanaugh. My father is James Cavanaugh.'

They were the words he had most dreaded hearing. The words that held the power to ruin everything. To shatter his plans and force him to break his vow to his mother. He heard them but he didn't want to accept them, shaking his head in violent rejection.

'No. I don't believe you.'

'Yes!'

Abbie actually stamped her foot to emphasise the word, wishing that it had more effect than the soft thud on the thickness of the carpet.

'Yes—believe it!'

'But they said his daughter was called Gail and she—'

'But I am Gail—Abigail—and…'

She lost her train of thought as the full impact of what he had said hit home.

'Who said that? And what else did they tell you?'

But if Malik had looked hard to reach before, now he was totally closed off from her. His expression was as blank as if it was carved from stone, his eyes opaque as if steel shutters had slammed shut behind them.

'Get dressed!' he snapped, waving an imperious hand towards the bathroom door. 'Put your clothes on—cover yourself up!'

'I'm perfectly well covered up, damn you!' Abbie protested in spite of the fact that just a few minutes before she had longed for the concealment of her clothes, wanting only to protect herself from the cruel burn of his furious glare.

But now she wanted the answers to some questions. Wanted—needed to know just what was going on here. What was happening? Who had said what? And why?

'And you can stop ordering me around! You might be able to dictate to everyone else, and your servants and subjects might have to do as you say—to bow and scrape to you because they have to, and it's off with their heads if they don't—but I've no intention of doing as you command. I want some answers and I want them now. I want to know…' she began again, but Malik wasn't listening.

'Get dressed,' he said again, grabbing her by the arm and bundling her across the room and through the bathroom door. 'Then we talk.'

A hand in the small of her back propelled her into the spacious room. A moment later her clothes were bundled up and tossed in behind her, flying through the air to land in a crumpled heap on the cream tiled floor.

'But…'

Abbie whirled round to protest, only to find the door slammed in her face.

'Get dressed!'

Even through the thickness of the door she could hear the danger in Malik's tone, the way his accent had thickened on the words, warning her of the vicious mood he was in. *Don't mess with me!* that tone declared. *Don't mess with me unless you're prepared to take your chance and risk the consequences.*

Just for a second she was tempted. But then the foolish impulse gave way to a rush of common sense and she silently conceded defeat. Better to be safe than sorry and right at this moment discretion was definitely the better part of valour. And at least at the moment she had the protection of the door between them.

'All right,' she flung at him from behind it, slamming home the bolt just to make extra sure. 'All right, you bully—I'll get dressed! But after that you owe me an explanation!'

Malik's response from behind the door made no sense at all and it took her a couple of moments to realise that he had flung something harsh and violent—and probably very, very rude—at her in his native language. But there was no mistaking the meaning of his next remark.

'Where explanations are concerned, the shoe is very definitely on the other foot. You're the one who owes me the explanation!'

'I think not!'

Security made Abbie feel brave and she edged closer to the door to fling her defiance from behind its shield.

'You're the one who seems to know what's going on—the one who called my father a liar and now me. And, by the way, it's boot! The boot is very definitely on the other foot…'

The words broke off on a yelp of panic as she heard his
snarl of fury and saw the door handle move with sudden vio-
lence. Nervously, she backed away but the bolt held at least
enough to make Malik reconsider his actions.

'Get dressed!' he commanded again, the handle still held
taut from the other side. 'Or else I'll come in there and do
the job for you!'

'You'd have to break the door down first. And the hotel
would want compensation for that.'

'And you think I give a damn?'

Even through the thickness of the wood Malik's tone
showed how little he cared about that. Hastily Abbie decided
that she had provoked him quite enough, her earlier foolhardy
defiance evaporating in a rush to be replaced by a shiver of
uncertainty.

'All right! I'll get dressed! Just leave me in peace to do
it!'

The tension in her spine and shoulders only eased just the
slightest bit when she saw the door handle click back into
place. He'd gone along with what she wanted—for now. But
how long would his patience last? How soon would it be
before he got frustrated and then what would happen?

With a sigh, Abbie stooped to snatch up her clothes from
the floor, struggling for the control she had lost so spectac-
ularly just moments before. There had to be some explanation for this—there just had to. She was going to take a few
moments to catch her breath, take stock, and then she was
going out there to tackle his High and Mighty Sheikhness and
find out just what was going on.

She wished she had time to take a shower. She felt grubby
and used, the memory of her pleasure in Malik's touch, his
kisses, tainted by the realisation that everything had not been
as she had foolishly imagined. How she wished she could
wash the feeling, the memory of Malik's caress from her skin.

But there wasn't enough breathing space for a shower.

Malik was already impatient enough; she could hear him prowling about in the bedroom, restless as a caged tiger. She didn't dare to provoke him any further than she had done already. She'd have to make do with splashing water on her face to freshen herself.

It was as she was doing just that that her numbed brain finally unfroze and jolted back into action, slamming home a realisation that made her thoughts swim.

She had forgotten about Andy!

In all the uproar that had followed the shock of Malik's reaction to her foolish words, she had forgotten perhaps the most important point of all. She'd lost track of the real reason why Malik was here in the first place—why he had ever come to England. She'd blotted from her mind the negotiations that had brought him to her family home to talk to her father.

But now she had remembered and she had to keep on remembering.

Lifting her head from the washbasin, she stared into her wet, pale face, seeing the shadows that darkened her eyes, making them cloudy and dull. Whatever else had happened, one terrible fact was true. For good or evil, Malik was still in control where Andy was concerned. He held her brother's future in the palm of his hand, to save or to destroy as he willed. She couldn't risk angering him too much or her brother would suffer the consequences.

Her fingers trembled as she pulled on her clothes, fumbling with the fastening of her bra, the zip at the back of her dress. It was impossible to forget the burn of needy passion that had seared through her as Malik had taken it from her, the way her body had trembled in need as he'd peeled the fine silk and lace from her aching breasts, exposing them to his hungry mouth and hands.

'Stop it!' she muttered to herself as she tried to comb through her hair with her fingers. 'Stop it now!'

She mustn't think that way or it would destroy her. It would crush her totally to remember just how much Malik had seemed to want her and how quickly he had thrown off all sign of any such thing. So how had he been able to totally switch off the passion that had had them both in its grip? Even now she still trembled from head to toe simply *remembering* how she had felt, her body a screaming mass of tormented nerves, while he was icy cold and in absolute control of every gesture, every action.

'Abigail...'

As if to prove her point, Malik's voice interrupted her thoughts, sounding a note of warning that once more what patience he had was wearing thin.

And she was Abigail now, was she? The warmth of 'Abbie' had gone, for ever it seemed, and her full name sounded harsh and alien in that exotically accented voice.

'Coming!' she called hastily, torn between wanting to stay hidden inside the bathroom for as long as she possibly could and the fear of the possible consequences if she challenged him by doing so.

Once again discretion won out over rebellion, the thought of Andy's plight sounding an extra warning note of caution not to make matters worse. She should be mending bridges instead of burning them—her brother's future depended on her.

Besides, there was little more she could do to make herself look respectable. The face that looked back at her from the mirror was white as a ghost's, with shadows forming like bruising under wide, dazed-looking eyes. Without the brush that was still in her handbag in the suite's sitting room she could do little to restore the tangled mass of her hair to any sort of order and had to resort to combing it through with her fingers, smoothing her palms over the blonde strands as a last resort.

'Abigail!'

The note of warning was back again. Any further delay was too dangerous. Wiping hands that were sweaty with nerves on the soft white towel, Abbie took a long deep breath, straightened her shoulders, lifted her chin. Swallowed hard and pulled back the bolt.

She fully expected that Malik would be waiting for her in the bedroom and so was surprised to find the room was totally empty. Not only empty, but the ruffled bedclothes had been pulled back over the bed to erase all sign of the wantonly sensual activity that had been played out there such a short time before. The whole of the room had been restored to such order that it seemed impossible that anything had happened there. It almost seemed like some sort of dream to remember just how hotly aroused both she and Malik had been.

If only it *had* been such a dream! If only it had all been in her imagination and now she could wake up and face the world again, shake off the last clinging remnants of the nightmare that had tormented her sleeping hours, put it to the back of her mind, knowing the monsters and the horrors had been only figments of her wild imagination.

But of course she couldn't. It had been real. And there in the sitting room was the dark physical evidence of just how real.

Malik was sitting in one of the big leather armchairs, his long legs stretched out in front of him, crossed at the ankles. He had fastened up his jeans and pulled on the black T-shirt that had been discarded only a brief time before, under conditions that made Abbie's skin burn to remember.

His elbows were resting on the arms of his chair, hands clasped together, his firm chin resting on them. He was staring into the distance as if his mind was miles away, his concentration on his inner thoughts intense.

And it was the consideration of what those thoughts might be that made Abbie shiver inside as she walked, silent on bare feet, through the bedroom and out into the sitting room to join him.

At first she thought that he hadn't heard her approach but then he flicked a swift, burning glance in her direction, black eyes glittering, his dark head not moving an inch. And the expression in those hooded eyes made her legs tremble so much that she was afraid they would give way beneath her.

'I'm here.' To her horror her voice shook disastrously as well.

That gleaming dark gaze swept over her once more, cold as black ice.

'So I see.'

One strong hand gestured towards the settee.

'Sit down,' he commanded.

He was too damn ready to issue orders and expect her to jump to obey them. Brief rebellion flared in Abbie, only to fizzle out again almost at once. For one thing she wasn't at all sure that her legs would support her if she tried to stay where she was. So she made her way to the chair opposite Malik's, carefully avoiding the settee he had indicated. The memories of the time she had spent on there, with him, and the feeling those moments had created in her were still too agonisingly raw, too terrible to remember. Just to think of them would destroy her ability to handle this talk and she strongly suspected that the next few minutes were going to be bad enough without adding any extra emotional pressures.

'Have a drink.'

Once more he gestured with his hand, indicating the glass of red wine that stood on the table to hand.

'Thank you.'

Abbie had to force herself to say it, not caring that she sounded gruff and hostile. She *felt* gruff and hostile, her skin prickling all over, her mind buzzing with nervous uncertainty.

It was impossible not to feel as if she had suddenly entered a time warp and that in a way they were replaying the whole evening, starting where they had begun tonight, with her arrival at the hotel and his offer of a drink.

Where they should have begun.

Perhaps if they'd started with a cool drink and even cooler words then the wholesale fiasco that tonight had turned into might have been avoided. If they'd actually *talked* before launching into a headlong rush for the bed then maybe this whole mess—whatever this whole mess actually was— would have been cleared up and she wouldn't have made such an appalling fool of herself.

Sitting down wasn't just that simple either. She had to remember that she was sitting opposite him and arrange herself and her clothing to create the right sort of impression—from his point of view. Not easy when the skirt of her dress was short and revealing and no matter how much she tugged it down it wouldn't go anywhere near covering her knees. Add to that the way that her tights had been ripped to shreds when he had tugged them from her legs and the fact that her knickers had not been in the bundle of clothing that Malik had tossed into the bathroom after her. They had to be still in the bedroom where she had kicked them off earlier after finding them hooked around her ankle, but she hadn't been able to spot them as she'd walked through. She couldn't cross her legs without Malik knowing that she was naked under the dress...

Shifting uneasily on the soft leather, Abbie took just as much of Malik's stony silence as she could bear. Then, nerves stretched to snapping point, her skin feeling raw as a result of that dark, intent stare that was fixed on her face, she gave up trying to be patient.

'You said you wanted to talk! So talk!'

Something dangerous flashed in the black depths of his eyes. Clearly Sheikh Malik bin Rashid Al'Qaim might be used to giving orders but he wasn't at all used to being on the receiving end of them. And equally obviously he didn't like it one bit.

But, whatever explosion threatened, he swallowed it down with the sip of his own drink and turned on her a face that, if not at all warm, then at least was not as furious as she had feared.

'Your name is Abigail Cavanaugh?'

'Yes.'

It sounded a bit spare and stark just like that and an imp of mischief fuelled by a strengthening swallow of wine pushed at her to add quellingly, 'The Honourable Abigail Cavanaugh, to be strictly correct.'

Of course Malik appeared neither quelled nor impressed, which annoyed her even more as she was left feeling foolish as well as edgy, irritated and vulnerable. All of which combined into a volatile mix of emotions that made her feel as if she was sitting on the rim of a powder keg, watching the fuse burn slowly towards her.

'You told me your name was Abbie, but in the past you have sometimes used the name Gail?'

'Yes.'

What was this, an interrogation?

'Abbie—Gail—they're both shortened forms of my given name. What's the shortened form of Malik? Mal?'

'No one shortens my name. I go by Malik and only Malik.'

He dismissed her flippant question with a cold-eyed glare, one that Abbie was sure had reproved courtiers, diplomats and any arrogant aristocrat who had tried to get above himself in the past. It left her feeling like a small child that had been soundly ticked off by an irritated parent and it was another uncomfortable feeling to add to the roiling mix.

'And you used to dye your hair black?'

That surprised her. More than surprised. It was a shock to discover that he knew anything about that. That he knew so much about her past. Why had he bothered to find out so much about her? And, on an even more uncomfortable thought, just who had been his source of information?

'Well?'

Her few seconds' hesitation had tested his non-existent patience again and the single word question had a real bite to it.

'Yes.'

She wanted to leave it at that but a sense that it wouldn't satisfy him pushed her into embroidering a little.

'When I was at school—boarding school—in the last year—the sixth form—I went through a Goth phase.'

She expected—and got—a frown of incomprehension at that comment but Malik clearly wasn't interested in the minor fashion details. Instead, he was intent on following whatever line of thought was running inside his handsome head and not deviating from it in the slightest.

'And in that year you had a friend—a male friend?'

But Abbie had had enough of being interrogated—of questions—when what she wanted was explanations.

'Just where are you going with this?'

'I'll tell you where I'm going.'

Malik reached for a jacket that was hanging on the back of a nearby chair and pulled a black leather wallet from the inside pocket. Opening it, he pulled out a piece of paper that he tossed towards her, watching as it fluttered on to the top of the table near her wineglass.

Abbie glanced at it, then stared in blank confusion. Finally, she picked it up and studied it intently, trying to make sure that she had actually seen what she thought she'd seen.

The photograph was six years old but she remembered when it had been taken. The last evening of the year at St Richard's boarding school. Exams had been over, the courses finished, and everyone in the sixth form had got together at a party to round off the year and to say goodbye. She and several of her friends had posed for the camera, all in a line, arms round each other's waists.

'Yes, that's me,' she said slowly, not really quite believing it herself. If she hadn't known then she wouldn't have recognised the girl who was in the middle of the group. Why had no one told her just how badly the dyed black hair had suited her? She looked totally dreadful, like some grotesque vampire from an ancient horror film. Gothic all right.

If this was the photograph that Malik had been using, then it was no wonder he hadn't recognised her from the image of her eighteen-year-old self.

'So what…'

A dawning memory stopped her in the middle of her question and she glanced back at the photograph to check.

Yes, she'd been right. There next to her, with his arm around her shoulders, hers around his waist, was Jalil. A wealthy young Arab, he had been sent to the exclusive private boarding school for the last year, to study and improve his English. Even though she had lost touch with him since, Jalil and she had become friends in the time they had spent together.

So was this what Malik was talking about? Was Jalil the male friend he had meant? She hadn't thought about him in years.

'Do you mean Jalil?'

'So what did your father tell you?'

Abbie's puzzled question clashed with Malik's cold demand and then they both fell silent. But when the look that Malik turned on her made it plain that he expected her to answer, not him, she made herself swallow down her pride and respond.

'He said that—that you had offered a way out of the mess that we—that Andy has found himself in. Is that not true?'

The horror of what that would mean, the way that Andy would have to stay in prison in Barakhara, made her shiver inside. It would be terrible if it was so—but clearly her father had got something very wrong.

But, to her amazed relief, Malik was nodding his dark head in agreement.

'It is?'

'I did offer your family a choice.'

Malik was measuring each of his words carefully. He was clearly back in the role of diplomat, well used to discussing matters of national and international importance.

'So then...'

'But not the one you appear to believe,' he continued ruthlessly, cutting across her stumbling attempt to speak. 'I have no intention of marrying you—and never had.'

CHAPTER EIGHT

So THAT told her.

Totally clearly, brutally honest, with no chance of any possible mistake. And how did it make her feel? Reluctantly, miserably, Abbie forced herself to face the truth.

She was relieved that Andy's fate didn't rest in her hands—but also worried that there had been no offer of hope for him. Shocked to think that her father might have misheard so badly and come to the conclusions that he had.

And cut right to the heart by Malik's reaction to even the idea that he might want to marry her.

Oh, admit it, Abbie, you weren't looking for marriage when you decided to come here!

Well, no, she hadn't been looking for anything—only for what Malik had openly offered. The wild sensual passion that had swept her off her feet and into his arms. But once she'd let her father put that thought into her head—for whatever mistaken reasons, he had thought it was the truth—she had come up hard against the sudden realisation of just how much she really wanted it, even though she had never allowed herself even to *dream* of the possibility.

In the deepest, most emotional part of her she had been singing, her blood bubbling with excitement. In her heart of hearts, she had acknowledged the disturbing, the almost shocking, the frankly terrifying truth that she had fallen headlong into love with this dark, proud, devastating stranger and her life would never be the same again.

But he had never suggested marriage, didn't want it. At least if he did want it then it was not with her. His reaction to just the word, the way he had flung himself from her and the careful, icy cold distance he had kept between them ever since didn't just tell her that, it slapped her right in the face with it.

He didn't want marriage.

He didn't want her.

At least not to marry. He had wanted her hotly enough when the idea had just been that she should warm his bed. But the idea of *marriage* to her had made him behave as if all the devils in hell were after him. She didn't need to be hit over the head with that more than once for it to sink in. The humiliation the first time had been bad enough.

'Who did you think I was—if you didn't realise that I was Abigail…?'

She'd made a wrong move there somewhere, taken a turning in the direction he didn't want to go and the flashing glare he turned on her told her that without any room for doubt. But, to her amazement, he followed her just for the moment, though his obvious reluctance warned that he was going to come back to whatever he had planned to say.

The terrible suspicion that she was going to like it even less than what had already gone before twisted the nerves in her stomach into a tight, painful knot that made it difficult to breathe.

'I thought you were the maid—or the housekeeper.'

Just for a moment a slow, wicked smile of memory curled the corners of his beautiful mouth, adding an extra twist of torment to the way that Abbie was feeling. Once, for a few brief shining moments, that had been the face she had seen, the expression that had been on his stunning features when he had turned to her.

She hadn't been deceiving herself. She'd seen that smile when he'd greeted her on her arrival and later, when that autocratic wave of his hand had cleared the room and they had been left alone together. For the space of a heartbeat he had shown her another side to him. One that was gone now, hidden under the cold, withdrawn mask that made him look as if his proud head was carved from marble.

'It was the apron that did it.'

The smile widened suddenly and Abbie couldn't stop herself from responding to it.

'It was a stylish piece of clothing, wasn't it? I'd borrowed it. I think it was the housekeeper's once—the previous housekeeper's—or the one before that.'

'I've never seen anyone but a servant wearing such a thing. So naturally—'

'Naturally—' Abbie put in sharply, her tone hardening, all amusement fading from her mind.

'Never seen anyone but a servant' he had said. Well, that put her in her place. No wonder he had flung himself away from her and from the thought that she might expect him to marry her! He was a sheikh—a desert prince—a ruler. And he would never lower himself to marry someone so far beneath him as a *servant*.

Taking a servant to bed for his pleasure, though, that was a very different matter. That was what harems had been created for, so that the king could take his pick.

So Malik had decided he could take his pick of the servants in the Cavanaugh household. And his choice had fallen on her.

But what would he feel now that he knew she wasn't the lowly maid he'd believed but in fact the daughter of the house?

Don't go down that road! she warned herself. Don't even risk it! What was she going to do? Hand him another knife and ask him to plunge it right into her already wounded heart?

'But if I had known who you were, I would never have touched you.'

And that answered the question without her having to ask it.

The burn of misery was so savage that she almost cried aloud with it. Hastily she reached for her glass and swallowed down another mouthful of the wine, wishing it would drown some of the pain she was feeling. But in fact it had the opposite effect. In her present, already emotional state the alcohol only heightened every sense to the presence of the man opposite. It stripped away the fragile, shaky defences she had built up, leaving every nerve suddenly raw and exposed.

It was as if she had been desperately short-sighted and suddenly someone had handed her a pair of spectacles so that her fight *not* to look straight at Malik, to blur the impact of his long, powerful body lounging at his ease in the chair opposite, was lost in a second. She became aware all over again of the strength of his lean form, the tightness of muscle in the arms exposed by the short sleeves of his black T-shirt. She couldn't miss the way that the light above his head gleamed on the blue-black silk of his hair, the polished jet brilliance of those deep-set eyes from behind their fringe of lush, thick lashes.

She followed every movement of his hands as if hypnotised, watched the way his mouth moved as he spoke and heard that voice as if in a dream.

'So my father had everything wrong? He's made a terrible mistake and…'

The words shrivelled on her tongue as she saw his expression change. Saw every last trace of the smile fade, the light of amusement die from his eyes. And knew a terrible sense of loss for the fact that they had gone.

'Are you hearing a word I've said?'

The anger in Malik's tone was like a slap in the face. She could only stare at him in confusion and doubt, blinking in shock.

He had said something while she was lost in thought and she had watched the movement of his lips but not heard anything of what had come from his mouth.

'I don't need to, do I? You've said all I want to hear—made everything perfectly clear!'

She'd got this far on a rush of panic, needing to get the words out. But now, to her dismay, her strength started to fail her and she could feel the shake forming on the last words as she forced herself to say them.

'It's okay. I understand.'

'No! You don't understand—not a single thing! You wouldn't be talking this way if you did.'

'But I do! My father got it completely wrong. There was no marriage suggested—ever.'

'No!'

In violent movement Malik flung himself from his chair and whirled to pace around the room for a couple of uncomfortable seconds, only coming back to stand facing her again when it seemed that he had got his uncertain temper a little more under control.

'In the name of Allah, Abbie! Listen!'

Something in the darkness of those eyes was deeper than ever before and the way that a muscle worked in his cheek gave away the fact that his jaw was clenched tight, which sent a rush of apprehension through her, her stomach twisting tighter in panic.

'I—I'm listening,' she managed weakly.

Her hand was clenched around the stem of her glass, clutching so hard that her knuckles showed white. She didn't want to listen. What she really wanted was to say, No—stop this now—I don't want to know…

But she didn't dare. If she feared what was coming, then she feared even more Malik's reaction if she tried to make him stop. It was like setting off to ski down the highest, steepest mountain she had ever known. She had already launched herself off and the movement couldn't be stopped, even if she suddenly spotted a terrible line of cruelly jagged rocks lying in her path. She was heading towards the inevitable and she could no more stop and turn round, back up the mountain, than she could tell her heart to stop beating, her breath to leave her lungs.

'Go on…' It was no more than a whisper. One that she doubted he heard, though he watched her lips move. 'I'm listening.'

'What *exactly* did your father say to you?'

Abbie didn't have to think, didn't have to hesitate. The words were etched on her brain in letters of fire. She couldn't forget them if she tried.

'He said—he said—"The Sheikh of Barakhara needs a wife." He has chosen me to be that wife. If I say yes, then the Sheikh will drop all charges against Andy and free him as soon as it can possibly be managed.'

'And you assumed that that meant that I wanted to marry you?'

'I—well, yes—it's obvious, isn't it? But of course it's not, now that I know you didn't say it and that Dad got things wrong, but…'

She was babbling stupidly and just the fact that he let her tongue run on with the nonsense, not saying anything, not correcting but simply watching her face, fixing her with the black intent gaze of a waiting predator, made her hand tighten even more on her glass, her throat drying painfully.

'But it seemed so, didn't it?' she croaked. 'After all, you're the—the Sheikh of Barakhara and you've come here to—'

'But I'm not.'

Malik spoke at last, his words cold and clear and deadly, dropping into the tumble of her answer like blocks of ice, bringing it to a stumbling halt.

'What?' Abbie managed, knowing she was gaping stupidly. 'What did you say? You're…'

'I'm not the Sheikh of Barakhara. My country is Edhan. Barakhara's borders adjoin those of my country and it is ruled by a member of my family—my brother. He is the one who wants a wife.'

'He…'

There was a nasty little crack and the bowl of the glass that had held the wine separated from the stem and crashed to the floor. The strength of her grip had snapped it and she winced as she felt the sharp point of the broken edge slice into her finger. But she couldn't react—couldn't move, couldn't think…couldn't believe. He couldn't be saying what she thought he was saying—he just couldn't!

And yet what else *could* he be telling her?

Her father had broached the subject of the Sheikh's proposal, not knowing that she had ever met Malik—and not knowing that she would immediately assume that *he* was the Sheikh who wanted to marry her. So he had been stunned, amazed but clearly overjoyed when she had answered his hesitating words with a wide, brilliant smile of pure delight and the declaration that…

Abbie's mind blew a fuse at that point, refusing to go any further, to think, even to consider what other horror Malik was trying to tell her now.

'Your brother?'

Her voice came and went in the most embarrassing way but Malik ignored the peculiarities of her delivery and simply nodded.

'My brother,' he confirmed. 'Half-brother to be exact. My father died when I was three and my mother married again. This time to the Sheikh of Barakhara.'

That brilliant black gaze dropped from her shocked, stunned face to the photograph that still lay on the table, a splash of wine spreading over its surface. And the way he looked at it told Abbie all that she wanted—no—all that she needed but had no *want* at all to know.

'My brother is now the one who rules Barakhara. He is the one who has the power over the laws of Barakhara and can say yes or no to the prison sentences they impose. He is the one who has your brother's future in his hands. He can show no mercy or the greatest leniency. And *he* is the one who wants you as his bride.'

'I don't believe you!'

The shrug of Malik's broad shoulders dismissed her protest. But it was the cold-eyed indifference in his eyes that shook her to her soul.

'Why do you think I asked you about Jalil?'

'Jalil!'

The ruined glass fell from Abbie's nerveless hands to land on the floor where the wine soaked into the carpet in a darkening puddle.

'You've hurt your hand.'

Malik's sharp eyes had caught the well of blood from the cut on her thumb and he was moving forward suddenly.

But Abbie couldn't take the thought that he might touch her. Her body was still stinging from the arousal that had flooded it. She felt barely under control, shaken to the core, brittle as ice. If he laid a finger on her she would go up in flames, splintering in the heat like the glass that lay on the carpet at her feet.

'Don't touch me!'

Whirling up on to her feet, she spun away from him, needing only to put as much space between them as possible.

'I was only going to…'

Malik flung the immaculate white handkerchief he had pulled from the pocket of his jeans in her direction, watching silently as it fell on to the arm of the chair she had just vacated.

'I wanted to help,' he muttered darkly as she snatched it up and wound it tightly around her wounded thumb, covering the thin line of the cut.

'Then help by explaining this situation to me.'

Abbie's chin came up, her mouth firming against the unwanted and far too revealing tendency to wobble betrayingly.

'My old school friend Jalil is the Sheikh... And he's the one who wants to marry me?'

'He's the one who put that condition on your brother's release.'

Malik's nod was curt and cold. The impulse to help had clearly died and he was once more the icily distant stranger he had become from the moment she had let slip those foolish words.

Jalil wanted to marry her? But he hadn't been in touch with her for years. And they had only been *friends*. She had never felt anything more for him. Certainly nothing like the fierce burning hunger she had felt for Malik.

But then she was forgetting that at one point Jalil had made a pass, had made it obvious that he had a major crush on her. She had thought that she'd let him down gently, but he'd acted as if she'd been callous and cruel.

'A condition I thought you had accepted. Your father phoned me earlier—before you arrived here. Perhaps before you even set out. He said that he'd spoken to his daughter about Jalil's proposal. That he'd sounded her out.'

'But that was...'

That was when I thought the marriage proposal had come from you, she had been about to say, but she couldn't let herself finish the sentence. How could she when it meant letting Malik know just how delighted she had been by his proposal? How much she had wanted to say yes.

How she had fallen head over heels, heart and soul in love with him.

She could only be so deeply grateful that she had never said a word about love to this distant, cruel-tongued man in front of her, his black eyes cold as ice. Letting slip the fact that she had actually thought of marriage was bad enough, to have admitted to love would have been the worst possible mistake. It was quite clear that Malik wanted no such thing from her and that she would only be fooling herself if she ever dreamed of him feeling anything at all for her.

If she could only find some way of covering her tracks, of hiding her stupid mistake, make him believe that she was as emotionally indifferent to this whole thing as he obviously was. That way at least she might emerge with some sort of pride intact.

But perhaps, just perhaps, Malik had given her just such an escape route with his talk of Jalil.

'And what if I say no?'

'You don't have the luxury of that choice.'

Malik's tone was flat, unemotional, as detached as his poker-faced expression.

'Your father rang to say that his daughter had said yes. My brother rang soon afterwards to know what was happening. Your agreement to marry has already been given to him. He is expecting you as his bride at the end of the fortnight. And I'm afraid that things will go badly for your brother if you are not there.'

Abbie's blonde head went back, her grey eyes widening even more as she absorbed this fact. She looked as if someone had slapped her hard in the face and Malik felt his conscience give an uncomfortable twist.

It was one thing keeping to his vow to their mother, quite another to go along with the crazy scheme the boy had come up with to use that vow for his own advantage. He had been assured that Gail Cavanaugh wouldn't give a damn about being used in this way—that she had always hated the way that her family had an elite name but not the money that went with it—death duties had seen to that.

Gail would do this, Jalil had assured him. She'd do it for the position she'd acquire, for the chance to save her baby brother from rotting away in one of Barakhara's jails. But most of all she'd do it for the money.

Gail would do anything for money.

But that was Gail. The woman in the photograph—the one with the dyed hair and the attitude.

This woman was different. This was Abbie—blonde-haired, grey-eyed Abbie. And Abbie seemed genuinely shocked at the idea.

'I'm sorry...' he began, but her laughter cut into what he had been about to say, stopping him dead.

She was shaking her head, sending that glorious blonde mane swirling about her face, one strand of it catching on the moistness of her lower lip and sticking there, making his fingers itch to reach out and brush it away. But he knew that, if he did, it wouldn't stop there.

If he so much as touched her then he wouldn't be able to stop. If he felt the softness of that lush mouth under his finger-tips then he would have to go further. He would have to trace its yielding contours with his hand, feel its warmth, slip into the welcoming heat beyond her lips, feel it close around his fingers.

He would have to give in to the urge to kiss her...

But then she laughed again, the sound even more jarring this time.

'You're sorry— Oh, don't say that, Malik! There's no need for that—no need at all to be *sorry!* Everything's worked out just fine. Exactly as I wanted it.'

'It has?'

He could hardly believe that he was speaking to the same woman. It was as if that laughter had transformed her face, wiping away the softer, more approachable mask that she had worn until now.

And what was under the mask was as hard as nails. The fine jawline tightened, her chin tilting in open defiance. Those delicate grey eyes sharpened, turning from mist into ice in one slow sweep of the long brown lashes. And the look she turned on him was pure ice too—a slow scathing survey that swept from his head down to his feet and back up again, her expression one of open disdain.

The woman he had known as Abbie had disappeared and in her place was a cold, arrogant individual he detested on sight. Abbie had vanished and in her place was the woman Jalil had called Gail.

'Oh, yes, it's quite, quite perfect,' she drawled now, giving him a smile that turned his blood to stone in his veins. 'Couldn't be better. You see, I only came here tonight because I thought that I'd managed to get a sheikh to agree to marry me. That was what my father had told me—and, quite frankly, I couldn't wait.'

She paused for a moment there, tossing back her hair and tilting her head to one side, as if she was waiting for him to speak.

But Malik had nothing to say. The bitter taste of acid on his tongue had burned away any words he might have managed, even the insults he could have flung in her face, to express the contempt he was feeling inside.

Surprisingly, the movement still hadn't dislodged the strand of hair from her mouth, but it didn't matter now. The impulse to move it, to touch her, had died completely. He would rather have picked up a live sand viper with his bare hands than touch any part of her now. If the truth were told, his own skin crawled to think of the way she had almost enticed him to take her to bed, to…

'But then I played my cards a little clumsily and you…'

A tight, dismissive little shrug of those narrow shoulders brushed aside what had obviously been the momentary disappointment of his reaction earlier.

'But now it seems that I can get just what I want anyway. I came here tonight, determined to get a proposal of marriage from a sheikh—and I wasn't going to leave until I got what I wanted. So don't feel sorry for me, Your High and Mightiness Lord Malik—on the contrary, you should be congratulating me. And you can thank your brother Jalil very kindly for his gracious proposal—and tell him I'll be only too happy to accept.'

Once more she paused, obviously for deliberate effect, and once more Malik knew that he couldn't find the words to express the way he was feeling. But he knew that his face must be saying that for him. His jaw was clenched so tight that it ached and his skin felt as if it was stretched across his cheekbones, pulled taut at his mouth and temples.

'I'll tell him,' he managed, forcing the words from lips that seemed to have become formed from granite. 'I'm sure he'll be very pleased.'

Jalil would be pleased. It would get him out of the mess he was in, maybe save his throne—even his life. He and this Abigail deserved each other. They were a perfect pair.

'You do that,' Abbie purred, turning a limpid grey gaze, a mock flirtatious smile, on his shuttered face. 'And do one other thing for me, dear Malik…'

Leaning forward, she touched a teasing fingertip to the corner of his clamped mouth, tugging it up into a suggestion of a curve.

'Smile for me, darling! Go on—try it! I'm sure you can manage it if you make the effort.'

But that was just too much. He couldn't take any more.

With a muttered curse in his native language, Malik grabbed at that tormenting hand, snatching it away from his face. Eyes blazing with disgust and fury, he glared straight into her taunting face.

'And why in hell's name should I do that? Why should I want to smile at you?'

'Why?' Abbie echoed, amusement ringing through her voice, her own smile growing as she did. 'Isn't it obvious, my darling? It's only polite to smile at your relations—and that's what we're going to be in the very near future. I'm going to marry your brother—and that means that from now on you and I will be very closely related.'

CHAPTER NINE

THIS couldn't be happening.

Try as she might, Abbie couldn't get her head around her situation. She found it impossible to believe that she was actually here, in the luxurious cabin of this sumptuous private jet, flying out to Barakhara.

'Flying out to Barakhara, to meet the Sheikh who wants me to be his wife.'

She had to say the words out loud to convince herself of the reality of them. But even then they had no real impact on her battered and numbed brain. They simply sounded like the most ridiculous gibberish, bearing no relation to reality at all.

'The Sheikh…'

She tried again and only succeeded in attracting the attention of the young female attendant who hurried forwards at once, a puzzled frown creasing her smooth brow, to ask if there was something that Madam wanted.

'No… Nothing, thank you! I'm fine.'

Physically, at least, that was the case. Since the car that had been sent to collect her had arrived at her home she hadn't wanted for a thing. She had never known such luxury—but it came at a price that meant she had also never known such total unease. She hadn't had a decent night's sleep since the truth about the Sheikh's proposal had become clear to her.

'Madam—we are about to land. If you would fasten your seat belt, please.'

The attendant would even have done that for her. She was already bending forward when Abbie stopped her with a softly raised hand. She had to do something for herself. Had to keep her independence for as long as possible.

But what would happen once they had landed and she was with Jalil—in his court—as his proposed bride?

Was she really going to do this?

Could she do this?

Abbie laid her head against the back of her seat, closing her eyes, listening to the change in the sound of the plane's engines as they circled around the airport, banked, flew lower and lower.

Did she have any choice? Jalil had been all charm and friendliness on the phone—but he had made one thing very plain. Either she came to Barakhara, prepared to be his wife, or Andy rotted in the country's prison for most of the rest of his life.

It might help if she remembered anything much about Jalil. But all she could recall was that he had been a smallish, very exotically good-looking boy—almost pretty, if the truth were told. They had been friends through circumstances, rather than through any real affection. Of the people in that final year of school, Jalil had been one of the ones she had got on well with at the time. But they hadn't really had a lot in common. And she had changed so much since then. The Goth phase, and with it the appalling dyed hair, had gone long ago.

She was going to meet a stranger.

She was going to *marry* a stranger.

And she didn't know how she could go through with this.

Oh, how different it would be if the Sheikh she had been forced to marry had actually been Malik. Malik, who had once been every bit as much of a stranger as Jalil now was to her, but who had so quickly become something else. Someone else.

'Malik…'

It was a sigh of longing as the image of Malik as she had last seen him floated in the darkness behind her closed eyes. Malik—tall, dark and devastating. Malik's mouth kissing her, Malik's long tanned hands caressing her body, removing her clothing with passionate haste.

'*No!*'

With a struggle Abbie forced her eyes open, staring into the shadowy cabin where the lights had been dimmed ready for landing.

She mustn't think of Malik! Couldn't think of Malik or it would destroy her. She had fallen head over heels for Malik in the first moment that she had seen him. Had fallen straight into his arms and into his bed—had fallen headfirst, hopelessly, desperately in love with him.

There, now she had admitted it to herself. She had let in the word that she had been fighting to avoid ever since that night in Malik's hotel when she had been putty in his hands, too hungry, too desperate for him to think of denying him anything.

She had already been in love with him then. Already totally given over to him heart and soul. When she had been with him she'd felt as if she had no mind of her own, nothing except what was his.

It was scary—it was frankly terrifying to realise how quickly and how completely she had fallen under his spell. She had never believed in love at first sight but she had no choice but to do so now. If Malik had reached into her chest and snatched her heart out of it he couldn't have taken control of her any more completely. She was his and there was no room for anyone else in her life.

But Malik didn't want her.

Malik felt nothing for her except the hot desire that had

flared between them. Desire that had ended so abruptly and had no chance of ever reviving after that one night that had gone nowhere in his hotel suite two weeks ago. The hope of love and a future that she had dreamed of had proved to be just that—a dream. And that was why she was here.

Malik didn't want her and so, with her heart feeling dead inside her, her thoughts too bruised and numb to fight, she had said yes to Jalil's proposal. At least this way she was rescuing her brother and Andy would have a future even if she didn't.

The sound of the engines changed again dramatically and a moment later Abbie was jolted in her seat as the plane landed with a bump, the screech of brakes and the rumble of heavy tyres over the runway.

They had arrived. The land outside the window, obscured by the darkness of the night, was Barakhara. The country where Malik's brother Jalil ruled, where Andy was still incarcerated in prison—and where she was soon to meet her prospective bridegroom. The man she had agreed to marry without even seeing him again.

'If Madam will come with me, the car will be brought to the plane.'

It was Sahir, the male attendant and bodyguard who had been taking care of her from the moment she had set out on her journey. He had been sent to her by Jalil with instructions not to let her out of his sight until he handed her over to her prospective bridegroom in the palace in Barakhara city. Abbie couldn't fault him for sticking to his job, but she was already beginning to find his constant presence oppressive and unnerving.

At least when she reached the palace she would be free of him. Free of Sahir, but handed over to a new sort of imprisonment... Oh, how different this might all have been if she had been coming here to be with Malik—to become Malik's wife.

Biting her bottom lip hard to fight back the sudden burning tears that stung at the back of her eyes, Abbie followed her escort out of the plane.

The heat hit her like a baking hot wall as she made her way down the metal steps to the waiting limousine and it was hard to catch her breath when even the air seemed to burn in her lungs. The space for the Sheikh's private plane had been cordoned off from the main part of the buildings, the formalities on arrival already conducted on board the plane, and so they were still some distance from the low building of the main part of the airport.

'Madam…'

The back door of the car was open, Sahir standing back with a faint bow. She would have to get used to this sort of treatment, Abbie supposed, the thought distracting her so that she slid into her place and leaned back, closing her eyes as the door slammed into place. It had barely done so before the car's motor roared, the powerful machine moving immediately, swinging away from…

There was something wrong! Very wrong.

Realisation and a terrible sense of dread struck at Abbie at exactly the same second. Instinctively, intuitively, she knew that this should not be happening.

Sahir had not had time to get into the car after her and, besides, she had not heard another door open and close or felt the change in the air-conditioned temperature in the back of the car.

Something…

'Sahir!' her voice was sharp with panic and concern as she sat up straighter. 'Sahir!'

'I'm afraid Sahir will not be joining us on this stage of the journey. He—has been relieved of his duties.'

'He…'

Abbie found it impossible to get any other words past the burning knot of fear that closed her throat.

She knew that voice. Knew it and had feared ever hearing

it again. Or did she mean that she had feared *never* hearing
it again? She didn't know and there was no room in the
whirling red haze of panic that was her thoughts to allow her
to think.

She was only aware of the fact that the voice—*that*
voice—*Malik's* voice—had come from just next to her,
sounding in her right ear.

Whirling in her seat, she confronted the man who sat
beside her.

Malik—and yet not Malik.

The forceful, strongly carved features were the same, such
as she could see them in the shadowy darkness of the car. She
could only snatch quick glimpses of his stunning face as the
car sped onwards, allowing her just moments of light as they
passed a window or some other form of illumination on their
way past the airport buildings.

The brilliant glitter of those black eyes was the same, the
same lean powerful form so close to her that the faint scent
of his skin and the tang of some citrus cologne tantalised her
nostrils. But this was no longer the sleek, sophisticated Malik
who had come to her father's home. Nor was he the more casually dressed but equally westernised male who had been
waiting for her in his hotel suite on the one night she had
come to him there.

Now, clothed more traditionally in a white *thobe* topped
by a loose black robe, his dark hair covered by the traditional
gutra, the male headdress, bound round by the cord *igal*, he
appeared much more foreign and dangerous, so outrageously
exotic and arrogantly masculine that his presence seemed to
fill the car and overpower her.

'M-Malik…' she managed, her tongue stuttering over the
sound of his name, her heart thudding high up in her throat
so that it was impossible to breathe.

'What—why…?'

The questions tumbled out on a rising note of hysteria.

'Oh, my…'

But her voice died there, crushed by the large powerful hand that was clamped across her mouth, strong fingers shutting off any sound she tried to make. She was hauled up against the strength of his body, her head supported on the hard bones of his shoulder, and burning jet eyes glared down into her widely fearful grey ones.

'No!' Malik hissed the word into her face, the ferocity behind them freezing her into panicked stillness, barely even able to breathe. 'Not a word! You will not say a thing—is that understood?'

It was almost too much to take in.

The beat of his heart under her ear, the purr of the car's engine, combined with the husky ferocity of his tone to intensify the effect of his accent and make the words almost incomprehensible. But she recognised the force behind the words and knew there was nothing she could do but give in—for now.

She had been going to scream. Malik had seen it in her face, in her eyes. She had been going to scream and that would have ruined everything.

There were still too many people around—too many people who might hear her. Or people who might recognise him, or the car, in spite of the way that he had insisted that the flag and any other identifying marks should be removed from it. If they were spotted now then they might not get away in safety.

And so he had had to act. Which meant that he now had her head crammed against his chest, his hand across her mouth, and the wide, shocked grey eyes staring up at him above the pressure of his fingers.

And it was pure torment.

He had thought that after two weeks apart from her he might have recovered from the madness that had gripped him when he had first met her. That he would realise that he had exaggerated the sexual allure of her body and the way it spoke to his own. He couldn't have been so knocked off balance by this woman. He'd known many women in his life—beautiful, stunning, glamorous women and they had enchanted him for a time—but only for a time. He had wined and dined them, enjoyed them, and had been able to walk away in the end without a single backward glance.

So why hadn't he been able to forget this one woman? Why had his days been haunted by memories, his nights by hot, erotic dreams from which he woke sweating and shaking, his whole body aching in frustration?

And it had only taken a single split second to have all those feelings rushing back.

So now, with the silky feel of her hair against his cheek and the scent of her body rising up around him, he knew that the two weeks they had been apart had not been enough—could never be enough. In the space of a heartbeat he was back under her sensual spell, with no hope of escaping if he tried.

And the hellish thing was that he didn't want to try.

That knowledge made his voice rough, his tone harsh as he crushed his hand against her mouth to stop her from betraying them both.

'Not a word—not a sound! You understand?'

Was that a nod or had she simply tried to free herself from his restraining grip? He saw the flicker of something in her eyes—fear or defiance?—and knew that neither of them could stay like this.

'If I let you go—you must promise…'

He didn't know which of them was more relieved when he eased his grip on her, allowing her to sit up. But the release was only temporary as she pushed herself away from him, turned her head in a swirl of blonde hair and opened her mouth…

It was impossible to get his hand back over her lips. She

was too far away, had turned too much towards the window. There was only one way he could hope to silence her.

He clamped his hands around her shoulders, hauled her back against him and brought his mouth down hard on hers.

And went up in flames in a split second.

Heat melted his thoughts, turned his blood molten in his veins. His head swam, his heart pounded and all sense of where he was or why he was there evaporated. He was hard and hungry, instantly wanting her with a ferocity that made a nonsense of his earlier beliefs that he could ever forget this woman or free himself from the sexual spell she had cast over him.

'Abbie…'

He sighed her name into her mouth as she melted under him. Her lips had parted under the onslaught of his, her tongue touching his, seeming to dodge away, but then, as if unable to stop herself, she met his intimate caress, teasing, inviting, tasting, taking…

His hands twisted in her hair, coiling the silky strands around his fingers to hold her head at just the right angle to increase the pressure of his mouth, his palms curving over the fine bones of her skull.

Her arms had folded around his neck, holding him close… so close. The soft swell of her breasts was crushed against his chest, her legs entangled with his as she lay half under him, almost full length on the back seat of the car, the ache and heat of his erection cradled in the tilt of her pelvis.

The lights of the airport flashed by unnoticed, the sights and sounds of the streets outside not reaching them as they lost themselves in each other, swamped by the primitive hunger that simply being together created.

He hadn't been alive for weeks, hadn't *felt* anything for days. His skin seemed hot and tight, his eyes were blind, his brain was lost in a wild explosion of electrical sparks. He didn't know if it was day or night, only that the woman who had haunted his dreams, tormented his days, driven him crazy with frustration and denial, was here now, with him, under him, her mouth on his, her fingers in his hair…

But then the car suddenly swung around an unexpectedly sharp bend, the driver lost control for a second, regained it almost immediately. But not before the rough, jolting movement had flung his passengers to one side and then back again, wrenching them apart, throwing them against the opposite doors.

'What the…?'

Malik bit off the furious outburst, clamping his mouth tight shut on the savage curse that almost escaped him. Or clamping his mouth shut against the temptation to reach for Abbie, to kiss her again—his whirling brain couldn't even begin to decide which.

This must not happen! He couldn't let it happen. His life was complicated enough as it was without getting entangled with some cheap little gold-digger who was already committed to his brother. He had come here tonight with the aim of helping Jalil—again—not making matters worse for him.

'I'm sorry…' Somehow he forced himself to say it. 'That should not have happened.'

'You're damn right it shouldn't have happened.'

Abbie had taken herself as far away as she possibly could. Which in reality meant just as far as the end of the seat, crammed up against the door. She had twisted in her place as well so that her back was to the window, her legs in their loose grey trousers forming a protective barrier between the two of them. Her hair was savagely tangled, her lips looked swollen from his kisses and her grey eyes spat defiance and rejection at him.

'It shouldn't have happened and it's not going to happen again!'

'Well, at least there's something we're both agreed on.'

'Both!' Her voice rose sharply in indignation. 'Both! I don't remember having anything to do with it. You pounced!'

'Only in order to shut you up!' Malik pointed out coldly. 'Admit it,' he went on, his voice softening slightly. 'You were going to scream.'

'And what if I was? Of course I was going to scream—I think I'm perfectly entitled to scream. I got in here expecting—expecting Jalil at least. And instead I find—I find…'

'You found me.'

It was a struggle not to let the amusement that was sneaking into his mind show at all. He knew that she thought she was aiming for the defiance and rejection she had shown earlier, but only wished she knew just how far short of it she was falling. She might think she was being fierce and strong and as bold as could be when in fact she looked like nothing so much as a small cornered kitten, hissing and spitting at some marauding tom cat several times as big as herself.

'I found you—and you immediately started mauling me!'

'I did not maul!' Indignation and pride drove any hint of amusement from his mind. 'You accused me of that once before, but let me assure you, I have never mauled a woman in my life!'

'Whatever you like to call it, it was not what I wanted! So let's be absolutely clear on this—I don't want you to touch me ever again without my express permission. I don't like you—I don't want you—and you're the last person on earth I want to be with right now…'

'Tough.'

Malik had total control of himself again. She might look like a hissing kitten but the reality was that she was much more of a problem than she ever realised. And she was in a danger that she couldn't even begin to imagine.

'I'm afraid you're going to have to put up with me for a while.'

'But why—why you? Why couldn't Jalil come to meet me? Why did he send you?'

Her voice stopped dead and Malik knew the moment that

the thought hit home. He saw it in the way the colour drained from her face, leaving it white and ghostlike in the dim light of the car. Her eyes opened even wider, staring at him in shock and fear.

'*If* he sent you,' she managed on a gasp. 'Is that what's happened? Where is Jalil? Does he even know you're here?'

CHAPTER TEN

'THERE'S been a slight problem.'

Malik's voice came from the darkness of his corner of the car, coldly calm and unemotional. His face was hidden by the folds of the *gutra*, concealing any expression from her, and his fingers were loosely linked in his lap, totally still. The very opposite of those ardent, caressing hands that had driven her to a frenzy of response only moments before.

'What sort of a problem?'

Abbie couldn't manage the same sort of control. Her voice went up and down in a most embarrassing way, echoing the erratic and fearful beat of her heart.

'What's happened? Has Jalil changed his **mind**? Does he not want to marry me after all?'

And if that was the case, then what would happen to Andy? After nerving herself to get this far, she couldn't bear it if anything went wrong now.

'The marriage deal is still on.'

If Malik's tone was meant to be reassuring, then it didn't work. In fact, it had exactly the opposite effect, sounding darkly ominous in a way that sent a miserable shiver running right down her spine. She wished she could move even further away from Malik's dark, malign presence but she'd edged just as far as she could go. The door handles were sticking into her back and her head was against the coolness of the window.

'Then why isn't he here?'

'He'd be here if he could.'

'If he could… What does that mean? What's going on?'

Panic rose in her throat. She had no idea what was happening; she only knew that she didn't like it one bit. Jalil must have had a good reason for providing her with a bodyguard but now Sahir was gone. What if he had been meant to protect her from just such a situation as this—from a man like Malik?

Twisting round in her seat, she grabbed at the door handle, yanking it hard, wrenching at it in desperation. And she didn't know whether to feel despair of relief when it didn't move.

'It's locked,' said that calm, controlled voice from behind her. 'They all are. Which is perhaps just as well. I hate to think what might have happened if you'd managed to open that just now. You'd have been dumped on a country road in the middle of Barakhara, without any idea of where you were or where to go.'

'Which right now would be preferable to being stuck in here with you!' Abbie flung at him, lying through her teeth and knowing it.

She suspected that Malik knew it too, though he didn't actually say it. But the way that one coal-black brow arched in mocking question and the cynical twist to his beautiful mouth made it plain that he was thinking along the same lines as she was.

'We're both stuck with each other,' he pointed out with a gentle tolerance that made her teeth snap together at the way it was so obviously faked. 'So we might as well make the best of it.'

'The best being what?' Abbie began but her sarcastic comment was broken into by a crackle of sound on the radio and a sudden sharp comment in thick Arabic from the driver.

The effect on Malik was dramatic. Leaning forward, he pushed aside the glass panel that separated him from the

driver and snapped out curt questions—or commands—
Abbie had no way of knowing—in the same language.

'What is it?' she asked sharply. 'What's happening now?'

It seemed an age before Malik answered her but in fact it
was probably only a few moments. But those moments were
long enough to twist her pulse rate up higher, making her
breath catch hard in her throat.

'Malik—what's going on?'

The expression on the face he turned to her was more
frightening than anything he might say. His jaw was held so
tight a muscle jerked at one side and the deep-set black eyes
were hooded and withdrawn.

'We need to get out of here. Can you ride?'

'Ride?' It was the last thing that Abbie was expecting and
she had nodded before she had time to consider just why he
might have asked.

'Yes, I can ride, but…'

She caught hold of Malik's loose sleeve, dragging his attention back from the sharp-toned discussion he was having
with the driver.

'But why should I? And don't tell me because you say so.
You might be king in your own country, but here…'

Her voice faltered suddenly as she realised that she didn't
really know where 'here' was. She had flown into an airport,
that was all she knew. Quite where Malik had taken her was
another matter.

'You don't rule me!' She managed to force a little more
strength into the words. 'You have to give me some explanation for what's going on. Some reason to go with you—
and it has to be better than "There's been a slight problem"
or I'm not going anywhere.'

Malik's sigh was a masterpiece of resigned exasperation.

'Do you ever do anything without arguing?'

'Not where you're concerned—no.'

To her amazement her rebellion earned her not the savage

reproof she was expecting but a smile. It was only a small smile, barely there in the curve of that sensuous mouth, scarcely lighting the darkness of his eyes. But it was at least a smile and not the frown and the flare of fury she had been dreading.

'I could order you to do as I say.'

'You could try!'

It was pure defiance, and she knew it. And so, she suspected, did Malik.

He could order her to do as he said and she would have to obey. It was either that or take her chances in a country she'd never visited before, where she didn't speak the language and had no idea at all where she was. If she looked out of the car window all she could see was darkness. Endless, impenetrable darkness. She didn't have a hope of finding her way anywhere in that. Even Malik was a safer bet than taking that sort of a risk.

'But you're right.'

'I am?'

She couldn't hold back the exclamation of surprise and disbelief, earning herself another wry smile and a nod of his proud head.

'I do owe you an explanation—'

He had to tell her some time, Malik admitted to himself. The situation was messy enough as it was.

'You do?'

Her astonishment was even more evident this time and, in spite of himself, Malik felt the corners of his mouth twitch again.

'I do. Believe it or not, I am not in the habit of abducting young women.'

'You mean you don't have plans to kidnap me and take me away with you to your desert lair to have your wicked way with me?'

In spite of the shadows in the car, he could see the way that her soft mouth quirked upwards and the big grey eyes opened wide, the flash of teasing mockery showing in them threatening his fight for composure.

'You've been reading too many novels.'

The vision her words put into his head had created erotic images that fired the carnal thoughts he had been clamping down on since that kiss. He could tell himself as often as he could that it had simply been meant to silence her—but his fiercely aroused libido knew different as the ache in his hungry body proved. It was torment sitting this close to her, inhaling the scent of her skin and not being able to indulge the need she woke in him.

'I've not been reading any novels!' Abbie retorted. 'There was nothing fictitious about that kiss.'

The realisation that she had been thinking on exactly the same lines as he had, remembering the heated potency of that kiss, did nothing to ease Malik's already uncomfortable state of mind—and body.

'I told you that was a mistake,' he growled. 'It isn't going to happen again.'

'No.'

Just for a moment he made the mistake of looking straight at her, looking into her eyes. Their gazes clashed, locked… clung.

This time a fine strand of blonde hair had caught on the long curving lashes of her right eye, moving, catching when she blinked.

This time he couldn't hold back. His hand moved on pure instinct, reaching out, touching the softness of the hair, her lashes.

He saw her eyes widen as she watched his finger come closer. She watched every movement, her mouth slightly parted, her breath snatching in and then stopping. Holding.

With infinite gentleness he eased the hair away, freeing it from her eyelashes and saw her throat move as she suddenly swallowed hard. Her breath snagged again, in the same moment that his heart thudded hard, just once, and he saw the pink tip of her tongue slip out to slick over her dry bottom lip.

Abbie...

Her name was a thought in his head, not spoken out loud.

What he did say out loud, clashing with exactly the same word from her mouth was:

'No.'

'No,' Abbie said again, reinforcing it with a shake of her head that broke the spell her eyes had had on him. *'No!'*

'You were going to give me an explanation,' she said a few minutes later, dropping the words into the silence that had fallen around them, broken only by the hum of the car's tyres on the road. 'And it had better be a good one.'

'There is trouble in the city—a riot. It was thought better—safer—to have you out of the way until things had settled down.'

'So Jalil sent you to fetch me?'

'Jalil has his hands full dealing with things there.'

He was deliberately avoiding the truth in his answer, and he suspected she knew that. Jalil hadn't spared her a thought. His mind had been only on himself—as always.

But it seemed that Abbie too was thinking along different lines.

'This—trouble... What will it mean for Andy? Will my brother be safe?'

'At the moment your brother is in the safest place possible.'

It wasn't the prisoners who were in trouble but the man who had put them under lock and key. Jalil's petty tyrannies, his greed and self-indulgence had always put him at risk of rebellion in Barakhara. Now it seemed that tensions had boiled over.

'So where are we going—why did you ask if I could ride?'

'Right now, the safest place is in the desert—the car will not take us where we're going.'

'You expect me to come with you just like this? To trust you—put myself in your hands...'

Abbie couldn't help it. The shiver that ran through her at the thought of being literally in his hands made her voice shudder too.

But not with fear. Never with fear.

She wasn't afraid of what he might do to her physically. That had never even entered the equation. But the emotional cost of simply being with him was something that made her heart clench in pain.

She'd hoped for more time to get over the vivid, violent response she had had to Malik from the start. It would take years, not days, to blur the memory of the way it had felt to be in his arms, to ease the sense of loss at his rejection. Whether she would ever get over the love she had felt for him was something she had to doubt.

And being here with him like this was only going to make matters so much worse. Already she had had to fight against the powerful pull of attraction. That kiss had made all the feelings she had tried to crush down reawaken. They had swamped her, destroying her ability to think, leaving her only able to feel, and her wild, foolish, stupidly passionate response had been the result.

So what was Malik's excuse?

He probably didn't think he needed one. She was just a gold-digger in his eyes and she only had herself to blame for that. She'd certainly dug herself right into that particular hole so that she couldn't get out.

'Or is it just that you snap your fingers and expect me to obey? I think you should remember that I'm not yours to command.'

'You're not mine…'

Malik let the sentence trail off without completing it, giving it a completely different meaning. One that added to the shivering sense of awareness so that she felt as if icy little footprints had been marked out all over her body.

'You're not mine, but if you were I would make it my aim

to make sure that you were protected and kept safe at this
troubled time. So, for this time, I will treat you as if you were
mine. I will do all that I can to make sure that not a hair on
your head will meet with any harm.'

'You—you'd do that…?'

She could hardly breathe well enough to get the words out.
Her heart was thudding high up in her throat, cutting off her
air supply and making her feel light-headed, her thoughts
spinning as a result.

Those words, spoken in a voice that sounded so deep and
heartfelt, the beautiful accent adding an extra note of sincer-
ity to the declaration until it sounded almost like the vows
one might make in church, made Abbie feel shaky all over
in a very new and different way. This time she no longer felt
cold. Instead she felt warm and safe, as if strong, protective
arms had folded around her, holding her close, keeping her
safe. She could almost hear those same husky tones declar-
ing the age-old promises, To have and to hold…in sickness
and in health…from this day forward…*Till death us do part.*

'You'd do that for me?'

The darkness in the car was almost complete, so that if it
hadn't been for the whiteness of Malik's headdress she might
have missed the way that his proud head inclined in a brief
gesture of agreement.

'You are promised to a member of my family and so, as the
representative of that family, it is my duty to ensure your safety.'

It is my duty…

Abbie could only be thankful that the lack of light hid
every trace of her reaction. Otherwise Malik might have seen
the way that the blood drained from her face, the sharp dig
of her teeth into the softness of her lower lip and the betraying sheen of painful tears that filled her eyes.

Every last trace of that wonderful protected glow evaporated from her, leaving her cold and miserable, as if she had
been caught in a sudden shower of icy rain. If he had actually

lifted a hand and slapped her hard across her cheek he couldn't have set her back in her seat with any more cold-blooded force, knocking all fight, all sense of hope, right out of her.

It is my duty...

Of course she was only a duty to him. Her own words, her defiant declaration that she had determined to marry a sheikh and she didn't care which one—Malik or his brother—had convinced him that she was nothing but a gold-digger and so unworthy of his concern or his respect. It was only because she was, as he had said, 'promised to a member of my family' that he was taking this trouble to care for her.

And she would be just creating a fantasy to even imagine otherwise.

The stinging pain made her want to lash out, putting a bitter note into her voice when she spoke again.

'So tell me, why do you spend so much time at your brother's beck and call?'

She caught Malik's brief frown that indicated that his nor-mally near perfect English couldn't quite cope with the phrase.

'Why do you act as his messenger—his advocate? I wouldn't have thought of you as his servant—'

'I am no man's servant,' Malik cut in, the bite in the words showing how her comment had caught him on the raw. 'But I made a vow to Jalil's mother—*my* mother—that I would care for my brother. His father died when he was only eighteen—just after he left the school you were both at—and our mother only lived a couple of years longer.'

He hadn't ever suspected that looking after his half-brother would be such a full-time occupation, Malik reflected as the car came to a halt at the place they had arranged to meet the horses.

Indulged from the start, Jalil had been a cosseted baby, a spoilt child, and he had grown into a weak and selfish young man. His grip on the reins of his country had always been loose but this latest bout of trouble was the worst he'd provoked. The young fool just didn't know the meaning of restraint—and he was incapable of listening to advice.

Abigail Cavanaugh might think that she had got the best of a bargain in winning Jalil's ring on her finger, but he doubted if the marriage would bring her any sort of happiness. But it seemed that she believed that immeasurable wealth would more than compensate for any lack of affection she had to put up with.

And of course there was the question of her brother's safety. Certainly, that had seemed the subject uppermost in her thoughts when she had heard about the rioting in the city. Was it possible that…

A sudden movement at his side distracted him from his thoughts as he turned just in time to see Abbie reaching for the door handle. Asif, the driver, had got out to talk to the men who had brought the horses to the rendezvous, and he had left the door unlocked.

'Oh, no, you don't…'

Reaching across hurriedly, Malik grabbed hold of Abbie's arm and hauled her back inside the car, earning himself a savage glare of fury as he did so.

'Just what do you think you're doing?' she snapped, twisting her arm this way and that in an attempt to break free. But all she managed was to get herself breathless and frustrated and rub her imprisoned wrist sore with her exertions.

The sight of the bruised redness on the delicate white skin was shocking enough to hit home like a kick in the guts. He couldn't control the roughness in his tone when he retorted, 'It's more a matter of what you think you are doing! Who gave you permission to leave the car?'

That brought her up short, her eyes flashing wild defiance, her breath snatched in on such a heaving gasp that the lifting and swelling effect on the rich curves of her breasts was dan-

gerously erotic. Malik felt his lower body heat and harden in
the space of a second, and the resulting fight with himself for
control almost made him lose his grip on Abbie's wrist.

Almost.

The situation was risky enough as it was. If word ever got
out that Sheikh Malik Al'Qaim had been seen with an un-
chaperoned western woman—and worse, his half-brother's
betrothed—Jalil's future wife—there would be the sort of repercussions that Abbie could barely imagine. They had to
take careful precautions—the sort of precautions that he
strongly suspected she was not going to like at all.

He was right.

When, still holding her firmly by the hand to make sure
she didn't leap out of the car in some wild attempt at escape,
he reached with his other hand into the side glove pocket and
pulled out a package, she watched him closely, eyes narrowed
in suspicion.

'Here, put this on…'

As he tossed it towards her, the parcel opened and the
contents tumbled out, falling to land in a swirl of black
muslin over Abbie's knees and lap.

'What—is that what I think it is?'

Her opinion was made plain in her voice, the cold fury,
the disgust in the words, but Malik chose to ignore the
implied rebellion and instead answered her question quite literally.

'If you think that the robe is an *abaya* with a *hijab*—a
headscarf—and veil, then yes, that is exactly what they are.
I suggest you put them on now, before you set foot outside
this car.'

'Put them on—you have to be joking!' Abbie's fingers
stirred the fall of muslin with reluctance, as if she feared just
to touch it would contaminate her. 'How dare you ask it of
me? It's an insult—'

'Only if you *see* the *abaya* and veil through Western

eyes—as an imposition and a curb.' Malik cut across her outraged protest. 'It can also be a form of protection. You are not in London or any western city now, Miss Cavanaugh. The men outside are not sophisticated bankers or CEOs. They are desert tribesmen with a fierce pride in their way of life, their traditions. To them, the *abaya* is a form of protection—and for you it will be the same. If you have any sense you will do as you are told.'

Seeing the way she still hesitated, the spark of mutiny that still burned in her eyes, the set of her mouth, he let his breath hiss through his teeth in a sound of pure exasperation.

'We do not have time to waste in delaying.'

'Then…'

'And you are not leaving this car unless you are wearing that! So make up your mind, Abbie. Before I make it up for you.'

The look she shot him from under her lashes was filled with pure venom, but she lifted her hand to demonstrate the way he still held her imprisoned.

'You'll have to let me go first.'

Then, when he still looked doubtful, unsure whether this was the prelude to another rebellion, perhaps an attempt at escape, she sighed and lifted her other hand, palm up, in an appeasing gesture.

'I promise,' she said. 'I give you my word. I won't fight or argue any more—not over this.'

Malik's mouth quirked at the corners into a smile that he couldn't keep back.

'That would be a first.'

Slowly, reluctantly, he let her go, knowing deep inside that the reason for his reluctance was not that he doubted her word or believed she would take advantage of her freedom. It was at once more simple and much more complicated than that. He didn't *want* to let go of her hand. Didn't want to relinquish the feel of the warmth of her skin underneath his touch, the fine strength of her bones, the softness of her flesh.

The truth was that he wanted to hold on for much, much longer. He wanted to expose more of that white skin to his hungry gaze, feel its smoothness underneath his caressing hands, kiss…

But if he didn't let go then she would begin to suspect just what sort of carnal path his thoughts were following and he could just imagine her reaction to *that*. Or, rather, he couldn't imagine this time.

And so released her. He moved his hands away and kept them away. But he couldn't tear his eyes away. Couldn't stop them from watching the swift, elegant efficiency of her movements as she pulled on the *abaya*, fastened the *hijab* over the pale glory of her hair.

Then she turned to him, the concealing veil still dangling from her hands.

'Okay?' she questioned. 'Satisfied now?' and he inclined his head in agreement.

'Okay.'

'But this is only for now. Don't think that because I've agreed to this it means I'm going to be a pushover from now on.'

'The thought never crossed my mind,' he assured her gravely, though the effect he was aiming for was rather spoiled by his mouth's tendency to curve even further into a smile. One that, to his surprise, Abbie met and matched with a quick, flashing grin of her own.

'Well, at least we understand each other on that.'

'So what made you decide to do as I asked?'

Abbie considered the question for a moment before looking him straight in the eye and admitting honestly, 'The fact that I have no other choice. I need to keep you sweet because you're the one looking after me. The one I have to rely on to keep me safe and get me to Jalil in safety.'

Pulling on the veil, she turned and scrambled out of the car so that she didn't see the way that Malik's face changed, the way that the smile that had warmed his expression faded at her words.

Jalil would have insisted on the *abaya* well before this, he thought as he followed her out. His half-brother might be a self-indulgent libertine who flouted the rules he had grown up by when his own pleasures were concerned. But he was a narrow-minded and unliberated bigot with regard to the way he felt that women should behave.

He was going to have to do some straight talking with Abbie about her situation and the young man she was so determined to marry, just as soon as he got the chance.

CHAPTER ELEVEN

ABBIE woke very slowly, very reluctantly. Yawning and stretching lazily, she winced as muscles she wasn't accustomed to using protested at the movement. Her legs ached and so did her neck and shoulders and for a couple of dreamy seconds she couldn't begin to imagine why.

But then her memory woke up too and with it came the recollection of what had happened the previous night, the thought jolting her upright in her bed, grey eyes looking round the room she was in, searching for the man who had brought her here. Searching for Malik.

He wasn't there.

Nor, of course, was she in a room. She had only a haze of memories of her arrival here, but one thing stood out so clearly. After hours of riding, hours of darkness, total darkness, with sand swirling in the desert wind, stinging against her face even with the protection of the veil, at long last, when the rising sun had turned the sky a burning red at dawn, they had come to this oasis encampment.

She had been barely awake by then. In fact, she knew that she had spent some of the journey asleep, the long hours of travel and the stress of the fearful anticipation of what the day might bring finally getting the better of her so that she had swayed in her saddle, her eyes closing in weariness.

Malik had noticed.

He had seen how her head had drooped, her hands loosening on the reins. He had rapped out a command that had halted their small caravan and then he had brought his own horse alongside the mare that Abbie rode and had touched her arm softly.

'Are you all right?' he asked, the husky concern in his voice almost destroying her completely. She was exhausted, lost, alone in a foreign country. It was years since she had actually ridden this far or this hard, though she would have died rather than admit it, and she didn't think she could go an inch further.

Behind the concealing veil tears of fatigue burned at her eyes and she struggled to blink them away as she nodded her head in response to his question.

'Can you continue?'

She wanted to say yes. Anything other than admit to him the weakness she was feeling. But she didn't seem to be able to form even the single word.

And then in a moment there was no need for speech. She hadn't even opened her mouth before Malik edged his mount even closer and was reaching out to take hold of her. Strong arms closed round her; powerful muscles bunched as he lifted her bodily from the saddle and brought her over from her horse to his. He settled her on the saddle before him and enfolded her in a supportive, protective grip.

'You are safe now,' he murmured in her ear. 'You can sleep if you need to.'

And the problem was that she did feel safe. Supported by the strength of those arms, with her head resting against the hard bones of his shoulder, she could close her eyes and lean back and feel protected. She even dozed a little, sleeping fitfully and waking to know the strength of Malik's hold on her, the scent of his body surrounding her. But the truth was that he could never protect her from the cruellest blows that attacked her heart.

He could never protect her from himself.

But he had kept her safe on their journey. And he had brought her here, to where they could shelter from the elements and from whatever trouble was still brewing—or had boiled over—in Barakhara's capital. Abbie had managed one thankful glance at their destination and she had fallen into a sleep so deep that she had no recollection at all of even being lifted down from Malik's horse or carried into the black woven tent.

She certainly didn't have any memory of being placed on this low, sofa-like divan and...

Another stretch, the feel of the sheets against...against her *skin*...made her sit upright in sudden shock.

Someone had undressed her before they had put her to bed! Someone—Malik—because surely it could only be Malik—had taken off the white shirt and pale grey cotton trousers, leaving her in only the lacy bra and knickers she wore underneath. Abbie's blood ran cold and then flooded hotly under her exposed skin until she felt as if she was in the grip of a fever. What made matters so much worse was that in her mind she could almost hear Malik's cool, intriguingly accented voice saying that he didn't know what all the fuss was about. Hadn't he seen her in far less—in nothing at all—on that night at his hotel suite?

But that was...

Abbie couldn't finish the sentence even inside her own head because she could almost see Malik's scornful expression, see the way that one jet-black brow would lift cynically as he looked her up and down.

What made the difference? he would scorn. Why was she now embarrassed? Then she had been only too keen to help him remove her clothing, had actively encouraged it.

But that was when you thought that enticing me into bed was also trapping me into marriage.

She could hear the words as clearly as if he were actually in the room.

Now that you know you're not going to get your way, you're not so keen to provide a strip show for me, is that it, hmm?

And the worst thing was that she wouldn't be able to find a way to answer him.

How could she tell him the truth—that yes, in a way, because she had had the hope that he wanted to marry her the time she had spent in his bed had become so special? That hope had made her offer her body—and her heart—so willingly.

How could she ever admit that it was because she had been weak enough, foolish enough—*stupid* enough to dream that maybe, if they did enter into an arranged marriage, he might one day come, if not to love her, then at least to care for her? He had had no thought of any such thing, and he had been totally upfront about that.

And she could have accepted that too. In fact, the truth was that she wished she had.

Flinging back the bedclothes, Abbie swung her legs out of the bed. A shining ivory silk robe, glowing with embroidery, lay across another divan nearby, obviously meant for her use, and she pulled it on to cover her near nakedness.

'If only I hadn't said anything.'

She said the words aloud as she paced restlessly over the beautifully carpeted floor, unable to sit still because of the discomfort of her thoughts.

If she hadn't opened her mouth, if she hadn't let slip that stupid, blundering comment about 'Every night of our married lives,' then she would have spent that night—and maybe many more—in Malik's bed, as happy as she could ever have dreamed she could be. She would have known his lovemaking, would have experienced the full knowledge of his physical possession, and she would have given herself up to the fullest of pleasures that he could give her.

And she wouldn't have asked for more.

But instead she had opened her mouth without thinking and so she had ruined everything. She had made Malik think that it was an 'all or nothing' situation when it was nothing of the sort.

If only she could have her time again. If only she could have another chance then she would grab at it with both hands, but keeping her mouth clamped tight shut this time.

If Malik would only show her once again the passion he had felt for her that first night, then she would meet it with a passion of her own, a passion fired and fed by the love she felt for him as a man until it would more than match the fire in his soul. Because that fire was still there. She'd felt it when he'd kissed her in the car and she had been unable to resist responding to him.

And oh, how she would respond if she got a chance to make love with him. If she only got a second chance she would grab at it with both hands and not lose out this time.

If she got a second chance…

But there was no hope of that—none at all. Malik had made it clear that he considered her forbidden fruit. She was betrothed to his half-brother and, as such, untouchable in his eyes. He had only kissed her because she had been about to scream, had only taken the kiss further because she had responded to him, her hunger feeding his. But then he had broken away and held himself coldly distant ever afterward. Even on the journey here, when he had lifted her on to the saddle before him and put his arm around her to hold her safe, his touch had been as cool and distant as a stranger's, unemotional as a doctor's.

He would never touch her again, not willingly. She was only dreaming to consider it—and, by allowing herself to dream, she was keeping open the wounds he had inflicted on her that first night. But how could those wounds have a chance to heal when she was forced to spend time with Malik like this in this desert hideaway?

Besides, she couldn't want Malik's passion and still hope to rescue Andy. The only way to help her brother was to marry Jalil—even if it tore her heart to shreds to do so.

It was late evening before Malik returned to the tent. Late evening on what had been a long, worrying, lonely and un-settled day for Abbie. The attendants that Malik had in-structed to look after her had been diligent in following his orders, attentive to any need she might have, but they couldn't—or wouldn't—answer any of the frantic questions that were pounding at the inside of her skull, tormenting her thoughts, demanding to know…

What was happening in Barakhara ?

What had happened to Jalil?

And what effect would that have on Andy's future? How would her brother be coping in this new upheaval—and were the effects of it potentially good or bad?

But, most importantly, most frequently running round and round in her head was the need to know just where *was* Malik? Where had he gone and why? And when—*when*—would he be back?

By evening she was almost in a state of despair and so when the tent flaps parted and Malik finally appeared in the opening she was beyond restraint, beyond even making just a polite greeting. All the pent-up emotion and worry exploded from her like champagne erupting from a violently shaken bottle.

'So you've decided to come back at last! Where the hell have you been? Do you know what time it is? How long I've been left here—on my own…'

'And good evening to you!' Malik snapped back, kicking the tent flap closed behind him and striding across the carpet.

As he did so, he dragged the white *gutra* from his head and tossed it and the black cord *igal* vaguely in the direction of the nearest divan before raking both hands through the jet-black hair he had exposed… He was dressed in a simple white *thobe*, topped with a long black cloak, both of which were wrinkled and dust-stained. Clearly, wherever he had been, he had not been dressing for show or as befitted his royal rank.

'What sort of greeting is that…?'

'The only sort of greeting that you deserve after abandoning me here alone all day long! I didn't even know that you had gone—and when I woke…'

'I left you a note!' It was a snarl of exasperation, an ominous sound of warning. 'I explained everything in that.'

'Everything! *Everything!*'

Abbie knew she should be heeding that warning tone but she was past caring. The long, mostly silent hours of waiting and worrying had stretched out her already taut nerves until they were near breaking point and she had to let her feelings out somehow.

'You explained nothing!'

Abbie grabbed the crumpled note from where she had tossed it aside only a short time before after reading it for the hundredth time. She didn't care if the fact that it was so close that she could just reach out a hand for it revealed how she hadn't been able to let it out of her sight all day long. Or if the fact that it was so crumpled gave away just how many times she had gone back over its contents. She *wanted* him to know how worried she had been. Wanted him to know the sort of torture he had put her through.

'"I have to go and find out what is happening…"' she read out loud in a voice that made her opinion painfully clear. '"You will be perfectly safe here until I get back. If you need anything, then just ask…"'

'Well, you were perfectly safe, weren't you?'

Malik's black-eyed gaze swept round the tent where the oil lamps threw a shadowy light over the carpets and mattresses.

'I see no signs of rape or pillage—and Omar tells me that you asked…'

'Oh, I asked all right! I asked to know what was happening but no one would tell me. And I asked where you were but no one would say.'

'I told them not to.'

It was positively the last straw, shattering the little that remained of Abbie's control and bringing her to her feet in a rush.

'You told them! Do you know how long I've been here—'

'Not now, Abbie,' Malik broke in roughly, bringing up his hands in front of his face in a brusque, surprisingly defensive gesture, physically cutting off the communication between them. 'I don't want to talk about it.'

'You might not want to talk, but I do. I—'

'I said *not now*, Abbie!'

If his fury hadn't stopped her dead, then the look on his face would have had the required effect. The same blind anger that had thickened his voice, roughening it at the edges was there in the blaze of his eyes, in the taut set of the muscles in his jaw. But it wasn't that that stopped her. Instead, it was the realisation that she hadn't really been looking at him since the moment he had arrived in the tent. Not looking so that she could *see* him properly.

But now she was. And what she saw shocked her right to the core of her soul.

The beautiful golden skin was drawn over the strongly carved bones of his face, stretched so tight at the nose and mouth that at times it showed white with a strain that drained all the colour from his cheeks. There were deep shadows under his eyes—shadows that were created by more than just tiredness, but spoke of a draining exhaustion that was mental rather than physical. And that glittering polished jet gaze now seemed clouded and dull under heavily hooded lids.

'Not now, Abbie,' he said again but this time in a very different tone of voice. Low and worn and shockingly flat, with no emotion at all in its husky notes. 'I don't want to talk about it now.'

It had been a hell of a day and he didn't want to talk about *anything*. He didn't even want to think. He would have to do that soon enough. He would have to explain everything to Abbie, tell her what this meant for her and her brother. He rather suspected he knew how she would react and knew deep down that that was probably the main reason why he didn't want to talk. He just wanted to…

'Sit down.'

It was Abbie who spoke, but she sounded so different that for a moment he almost didn't recognise it.

'Sit down before you fall down. I'll get someone to bring you a drink.'

She was heading towards the tent entrance as she spoke but he put out a hand to stop her as she would have gone by.

'No. I'm sure you must have some water and that's all I need.'

'Of course.'

As she changed direction, Malik threw himself down on to one of the divans and rested his aching head thankfully against the soft cushions that were piled up around him. He closed his eyes and let himself be completely still and silent at last.

This was what he had dreamed of on the journey back to the oasis. The one thing that had kept him going had been the thought that, at the end of the long, tiring ride he would be here, in the peace and stillness of this tent. He had even allowed himself to imagine…

'Your water.'

Reluctantly he opened his eyes to see Abbie standing before him, holding a glass of water out to him.

'*Shokran*—Thank you…'

He took it, gulped down the cool liquid thankfully, but barely even noticed the clear taste of the water, the way it soothed his parched throat. Instead, his whole attention was focused on the woman who stood before him.

The woman he had been unable to get out of his mind all day long. The woman who had been at the forefront of his thoughts as he rode away from the oasis. The woman who had still been there as he rode back, with the news he had to tell her fretting at his brain. He had once, foolishly, allowed himself to imagine, to dream, how it would be if she was waiting for him to come back to her—to come home to her...

Malik's hand tightened convulsively around the glass until his knuckles showed white.

He'd actually allowed himself to picture how it might feel if he had a woman who loved him waiting for him—a woman he loved in return. And in his tiredness, the lowness of his mood, he'd let himself dream that Abbie might be that woman.

And now, here she was, standing before him, like his dream brought to life. She was looking more beautiful than he had ever seen her. The long blonde hair hung loose and flowed over her shoulders like gilded water. The ivory silk robe flowed too, skimming over the slender length of her body, clinging a little at the curves of her hips, the swell of her breasts in a way that made his mouth dry in spite of the water he had just drunk.

He had never wanted a woman in his life as much as he wanted Abigail Cavanaugh. He wanted her so much that his body ached with it—hell, his *soul* ached with the hunger she created in him.

If only she hadn't been who she was.

That night in his hotel suite, he had been on the edge of one of the greatest sexual experiences of his life. One of the greatest *experiences of his life*, with no qualification whatsoever. And then she had come out with those six shocking words: 'Every night of our married lives' and it had felt as if a grenade had exploded right in his face.

He couldn't touch this woman. She was the woman his brother had wanted as a wife and honour demanded that he walk away from her. He had tried, but he hadn't been able to get her out of his mind. He'd even used the fact that there was trouble in Barakhara as an excuse to come back into her life, to see her just one more time. Even though he'd known that it would put him through a torment of frustration just to be with her.

That and the fact that Jalil obviously hadn't cared whether his prospective bride could reach the capital in safety or not. Someone had had to ensure that she came to no harm between the airport and the palace.

At least that was what he had told himself. He knew that the truth was that he had just been hunting for an excuse to see her again.

But now...

Now everything was different. Or was it?

A lot had changed—changed irrevocably. Abbie was no longer forbidden to him. And he knew that he would do anything for another chance to spend even one night with her. To know the intimate delights offered by that glorious body, to bury himself in her, sate himself...

Hell, who was he trying to fool? How could he ever sate himself on this woman in one night?

'Why are you staring at me like that?'

Abbie was watching him warily, her grey eyes narrowed, a faint frown creasing the fine skin between her delicate brows.

'Was I staring? Forgive me.'

He could only pray that she would believe the huskiness of his voice, his struggle to compose himself and focus on the present and not his fantasies of a future, were the result of tiredness at the end of a long day.

'What has happened, Malik?'

Clearly he hadn't convinced her. Or did he mean that he

had managed to convince her only too well? If the truth was told, he didn't know the answer to that question and he didn't feel at all like trying to find it.

'Could I have some more water?'

He was dodging the issue and, to judge from the look she gave him, Abbie was only too well aware of the fact. But what was he to do? Blurt out the stark facts without any preparation?

But at least she took the glass he held out again and walked away from him to refill it without a word.

Malik had to smother the groan of response that rose to his lips as he watched the sensual sway of her hips, the way the ivory silk slid over the curves of her buttocks, and felt raw, brutal need claw at his guts. He wanted this woman so much that it was agony to sit here, watching her, and do nothing. And he wanted her more than ever today, wanted her as a way of asserting life in the face of...

Images flew up before his mind's eye, images he didn't want to see, couldn't bear to imagine, and he put his hands up to his face, covering his eyes, in an attempt to block them off.

'Are you ill?'

'Fine.'

Malik slid his hands up over his face and out at his temples, raking his fingers through his hair in an attempt to disguise the way he was feeling. The muscles at the back of his neck were tight and sore and he rubbed at them in an effort to ease the tension.

'You don't look fine. Do you have a headache?'

'*Naam.*' He was beyond finding even the simple English word as he nodded his head in agreement.

Why did she have to be this way now? Why did her voice have to be soft, concerned? Her eyes, when they met his as he raked both his hands through his hair, were shadowed with thought, a very different frown now showing between the pale brows. This Abbie awoke feelings, needs, that he was in no mood to struggle against.

Why couldn't she be the spiky-voiced woman who had greeted him with indignation on his arrival just a short time before? The woman whose sharp-eyed glare and even sharper tongue had made him long for silence and some time of peace in which to adjust. That woman…

Oh, who was he fooling? Not even himself!

This woman made him want to gather her close, hold her tight, but kiss her softly. Kiss away that look of anxiety, close the soft mouth against the words of concern that rose to her lips…

…And take her to bed.

The other woman, the other Abbie, made him want to grab at her, shake the anger from her face, crush the accusatory words from her lips and back down her throat. He wanted to kiss those blazing eyes closed against the burn of anger, smother her irritation under her closed eyelids…

…And take her to bed.

'I'd have something for that if I knew where my luggage had been taken.'

The sudden return of a touch of tartness to her tone made his mouth twist into a wry smile.

'The driver had orders to deliver it to the palace. It will be quite safe.'

'I'm sure it will, but in the meantime…'

She pushed the glass into his hand and then moved round the divan, coming up close behind him.

'What are you doing?' Malik demanded as soft fingers brushed the hair away from his neck, probed the muscles gently.

'Trying to help you with your headache. Hmm—your muscles are tight here… Sorry, did that hurt?'

'No.'

It came through gritted teeth. He'd not been able to hold

back the groan in response to the feel of her fingers on his skin, the warmth and softness of her touch. The scent of her body surrounded him, clean and sweetly feminine, setting his heart pounding as he inhaled.

Her touch was working magic. Under the massage, the tightness in his neck and shoulders was beginning to ease. If he admitted to the truth, then it was easing far too quickly so that his brain seemed to have melted along with it. If he leaned back just slightly then his head was resting against the warmth of her body, pillowed on her breasts, sinking into their lush contours. He could feel each breath she took, hear the beat of her heart, the pulse of her blood through her veins.

It was agony and ecstasy all at once. Ecstasy because of the almost sinful pleasure he felt, the sensual enticement that whispered to him to stop thinking, just feel, to abandon himself to the pleasure that the woman promised.

But the agony that slashed through that feeling was both physical and mental. Physical because he was hard and swollen, aching for release, mental because he knew he had to deny the bite of that need, and by denying make it so much more unbearable.

He couldn't relax until he had told her. Couldn't do anything for himself, indulge himself in any way—do *anything*—until she knew the truth.

She had to know.

'Careful.' Abbie's voice came from behind him, the lighter, almost teasing note shocking in contrast to the force of his thoughts. 'You almost relaxed then.'

'Abbie…' Malik began and knew that his tone had given away his mood in the space of a heartbeat.

The soothing fingers stumbled, paused, began again, but less confidently this time. The rhythm of her movements was less fluid, slightly awkward, in a way that showed how her mind was not on what she was doing.

'I have something to tell you.'

Was it easier to tell her when he couldn't see her face?

One part of him wanted—needed to see how she reacted. Another wanted to do anything but watch what happened to her face when he told her the news.

But already he'd hesitated too long. Her fingers might continue to move but their actions were mechanical, uninvolved, and he could feel the way she was holding herself, taut with apprehension and uncertainty, needing to know.

'What is it?' she asked when he couldn't find the words. 'What's happened?'

Find the words! Malik almost laughed out loud at the thought—except that this was no laughing matter at all. There were no words other than the ones that told it straight.

'Malik… What happened?'

He drew in a deep breath, forced it out.

'There was an accident—Jalil—Jalil's dead.'

CHAPTER TWELVE

JALIL'S dead.

The words hit like a blow in Abbie's face, stopping her fingers, stilling her breath.

Had Malik said...?

She couldn't have heard right, could she?

How could Jalil be dead?

'Abbie, did you hear what I said?'

Malik had moved on the divan, turning to face her, and the intent set of his face, the blaze of his black eyes told her that, whatever else had happened, he had most definitely meant what he had said.

'I heard—but...but I was going to marry him!'

A hundred thoughts ran through her head, thoughts she couldn't link together or make any sense of.

How could Jalil be dead?

When?

Had this terrible thing happened today?

And what did this mean for the future? For her? For Andy?

But then the shock cleared from her eyes and she looked into down into Malik's dark face, into those bleak black eyes, and her whole mood changed in a rush.

'He was your brother. I'm so sorry...'

Just for a second, Malik's proud head went back, his eyes closing briefly. When he opened them again it was as if he had brought shutters down behind them, so that his gaze was closed and opaque, impenetrable. Obviously she had over-stepped some line she hadn't been aware of, treading where she wasn't supposed to go.

'What—what happened?' she managed hesitantly, unsure if this too would be a step too far, one that might dramati-cally break his calm and bring down anger on her head.

But Malik answered evenly enough, though with a catch in his voice that tore at her vulnerable heart where he was concerned.

'Because of the mood in the city, Jalil decided to get out of there for a while and a helicopter seemed the easiest way to do that. My—he insisted on taking the controls himself and he is—was—never the best of pilots. Something went wrong and the helicopter crashed into the sea...'

'He might not have—died.'

Unable to bear the flat, desolate tone of his voice, Abbie rushed in to try and offer hope.

'They might have got out...'

Her voice, and the small hope, faded as she saw Malik shake his head sombrely.

'They found the bodies. He's gone.'

'Oh, no—'

And she had been nagging at him for leaving her alone!

Jalil had been his brother—how would she feel if this had happened to Andy...?

Impulsively Abbie flung herself down on the divan beside Malik and caught hold of his hand. She didn't care that he had made it plain he didn't want her sympathy; she couldn't hold it back. She'd had to say this, but now, seeing the barriers he'd put up, she would have to accept that he didn't want to talk and that she needed to change the subject.

'I really am sorry.'

She sounded it too, Malik acknowledged. And there was

a softness in her eyes, in her face, that reached through the wall he had tried to build around himself. He had needed that wall because he knew she had only seen his brother as a sheikh—*the Sheikh* she had declared it was her ambition to marry. He hadn't expected any sort of sympathy at all, so he'd pulled away, mentally, when she'd offered it, taken aback when he'd been expecting something else. When he'd anticipated that her very first question would be…

'Where does this leave me?'

Okay, so it hadn't taken her too long to get round to it. And somehow the disappointment in knowing that she'd just been getting there was all the worse for the momentary belief that she might actually have cared.

'Well, the wedding's off.'

The grim humour worked where he couldn't find anything else to say. And Abbie actually flinched away from it, grey eyes reproachful.

'I meant where does it leave Andy?'

Of course. Her brother.

Well, he could understand that, couldn't he? Hadn't he always feared that one day Jalil would do something so stupid that there would be no turning back…? But if there had been a single chance that his brother could be helped, he would have moved heaven and earth to do so.

But what was Abbie prepared to do to rescue her brother? Were her actions solely selfless, or was she already looking for Jalil's replacement?

'There'll be a new sheikh in Barakhara—someone to take Jalil's place.'

As he had suspected, that brought a new spark to her eyes, her head lifting, expression lightening. The small smile that touched her mouth had the force of a double-edged sword slicing into his guts.

Was it a smile of relief—or triumph? Privately he cursed the fact that he hadn't seen her face when he had first told her about Jalil. If he had been watching her expression then, he would know more about the way her mind was working.

'Who is the new sheikh?'

Didn't she know? Couldn't she guess?

'Why do you want to know, *habibti*?'

'I need to know who to go to—who to talk to.'

He reached for her hand, stroked soft fingers down over her palm, watching her watching him, eyes wide, irises huge and black against a tiny rim of grey. And he knew the terrible temptation to test her, to find out just how far she really would go. The need to know was like a sore tooth, like a wound, that he just had to probe, to dig into, to scour right to its core. To root out and exorcise the corruption that was in it.

'Are you looking for another sheikh to marry, hmm? Will you throw yourself at his feet—into his bed? Into my bed?'

He slid the question in as if it was a stiletto slipping between her ribs, into her heart.

'Your…?'

She'd been looking down at their linked hands, long lashes lowered so that they lay like soft crescents on the fine slant of her cheekbones, but now her gaze flew upwards again to clash with his, lock—and hold.

'*Your* bed?'

'Of course my bed.'

Malik tightened his grip on her hand, exerting just enough pressure to warn her that he could hold her prisoner, that he could control her if he wanted. Not enough to hurt—but enough to caution her to be very careful in what she said next. And he saw the flicker in those grey eyes that told him she understood—on the very deepest level.

'Didn't you realise? That as Jalil's brother—as his one living relative—I am the only man who can inherit his throne? His country will unite with mine and I will rule them both.'

'Then you—you will have power over Andy?'

'I'll have control over everything in Barakhara.'

The hand he held jerked, just once, in his grasp, and her eyes were torn from his, her gaze dropping to stare down at the spot where their fingers linked together.

But not before he had caught the second, flashing smile that she couldn't control. And this was a smile that he recognised. He'd seen it before on that night in his hotel room—in his bed—when she had thought that she had him—that she had him caught snug and tight, wrapped in her beguiling spider's web.

It was a smile of pure feminine triumph. And suddenly he felt that he knew just what some poor misguided fly must feel to know that it was trapped and the female predator was bearing down on it, about to eat it alive.

He should leave right now. Back out—put an end to this before it had started. But everything that was male in him protested at the thought of never ever knowing this woman physically. Only a few moments ago he had told himself that he would do anything just to enjoy that glorious body once in his life.

And tonight, after all that had happened, he needed that release, that assertion of *life*, so much more than ever before.

'Then what can I do to persuade you to be merciful?'

'I would have thought that you would find that only too easy.'

He must be more tired than he had thought, Malik thought, cursing his unguarded tongue that had let the words slip out before he had had time to consider the wisdom of opening his mouth. But he had to know just how far she would go.

'And what do you mean by that?'

'Oh, I think you know, *sukkar*,' Malik drawled. 'After all, I have firsthand experience of just how…persuasive…you can be. So persuade me.'

'You want…'

Abbie couldn't believe what she was hearing. And she had

no idea at all just what she should feel. She had thought that she had lost her only chance to help Andy—and now she was being offered it all over again, but at what a cost!

'You want…'

'I want you.'

It was a flat, emotionless statement, one that stabbed right to Abbie's already wounded heart like the cruellest blade. She had always known he didn't care for her, but to hear it declared in this cold, blunt way was almost more than she could bear.

'I've always wanted you. More than any woman I've ever met. And I'm prepared to pay any price to have you in my bed.'

'Pay any price!' Abbie echoed, her voice sharp with incredulity. He wouldn't be *paying* anything! 'You mean, you'll set my brother free?'

'I'll do anything you ask, if you offer me what you were prepared to give Jalil. Come to my bed—'

'As—as your concubine—your mistress?'

She had to force the words out, her voice was shaking so badly and her tongue felt as if it had turned to solid ice.

Malik shook his dark head, refuting her words.

'No. As my wife.'

His *wife*. If he had taken hold of the invisible dagger that was in her heart and twisted it brutally, it couldn't have hurt her any more. He didn't know what he was asking. He *couldn't* know.

Loving him as she did, the thought of being his wife was like a dream come true—but not in a cold-blooded, cruel bargain like this!

'I—I can't…'

She wished she could make herself get up and move away but her mind seemed to have lost control over her limbs. They wouldn't move at all and she was sure that if she tried to stand up her legs wouldn't have the strength to support her. So she had to stay where she was, with her face so close to his, the black eyes burning into hers as he held her gaze with his.

'Why not ?' Malik demanded, low and hard. 'Surely one sheikh is as good as another. You wanted to marry a sheikh—I'm offering you marriage to one. Marriage, your brother's freedom—a life of luxury beyond your wildest imaginings—and every night of your life spent in my bed. How can you refuse?'

How *could* she refuse? Abbie could find no way even to answer herself as the question spun round and round inside her head. She'd vowed to do anything to help Andy, anything at all, but right now even her brother's future wasn't what was uppermost in her mind. It was her own deepest, most secret longing that was pushing her in the direction of the wildest, most impossible decision she had ever made.

…every night of your life spent in my bed.

She'd said she'd take one chance if it was offered—and here it was. Here Malik was offering the one thing that tempted her—the thought of really making love with him. And she couldn't walk away from that.

She had to take it. But she didn't dare to take it.

The risks were too great. It would hurt too much. But it would hurt far more to turn away.

'Abbie…' Malik prompted softly, drawing her eyes to him again.

The darkness that surrounded the tent was complete; there was no sound from the other men, the horses, the camels, outside the tent. They must all be asleep by now, it was already so late.

They might be alone out here in the desert, under the cool light of the moon. And here, in this tent, Malik was not the Sheikh of Edhan and Barakhara. Here he was just a man. A man who had endured a day from hell and bore the signs of it etched on his face, along with the shadows thrown over it by the guttering lamplight.

She longed for a kiss from that shockingly sensual mouth, and all she had to do was to bring her face just a little closer to his and she could take that kiss for herself—take it and see where that led her, what the consequences were.

She wanted to touch, and all she had to do was to ease her wrist from the loosened grasp of his fingers and reach out, touch his hair, touch his face...

But even as the thoughts slipped into her head they were sent flying right out again as Malik moved the hand that held her wrist and a sudden unexpected pain forced a small cry from her mouth.

'What?'

Malik turned her hand in his so that the lamplight fell directly on to her wrist and a rough curse in his own language escaped him at what he saw. The embroidered cuff of the robe had slipped back, exposing the pale flesh marred by a bruise that was already darkening to purple.

'Last night... In the car...'

Abbie blinked in shock at the change in the sound of his voice. It was as if another man had taken Malik's place, a man whose taunting, seductive tone had vanished and in its place was a tenderness that went straight to her vulnerable heart.

This time when his fingers touched the softness of her skin, they were infinitely gentle, meant to soothe rather than hurt. And the delicate path traced by those square, strong tips made her shiver in instant response.

'Forgive me,' he said huskily, lifting her bruised wrist to his mouth.

When he pressed his lips, warm and devastatingly soft, against the reddened skin, it was like setting a match to tinder-dry wood, starting a tiny electrical spark that raced along the lines of her nerves, heating the blood in her veins as it went, setting the whole of her body alight and alive with wanting.

As just as a few moments earlier she hadn't been able to hold back the quick smile of relief and delight at the thought that Malik was the one who had Andy's future in his hands, so now she couldn't rein in the yearning need that possessed her whole body simply at his touch.

'Malik…'

His name escaped her on the softness of a breath because even now she couldn't believe what she was going to say. She only knew that she had to say it. She could never live with herself if she didn't.

'This marriage that you're offering—with every night of my life spent in your bed… Show me what it would be like—and then I'll decide.'

His smile was like the sun coming up, the dawn of a brand new day, the start of something wonderful.

'Your wish is my command…'

And, leaning forward, he took her mouth in a slow, lingering kiss that seemed to draw her soul right out of her body and into his hands, to do with as he wanted. His lips were firm but gentle, the slow, provocative sweep of his tongue along the line of her mouth an invitation and a question all in one. And as soon as she knew the unique taste of him against her mouth it was as if she had taken a wild, abandoned gulp of the most potent spirit, with a fierce, intoxicating effect that flooded her veins with fire, seared her skin, turned her blood to white heat so that it felt as if her bones were melting in the burn of it.

But the wildest burn of all was between her thighs, at the very core of her femininity, where the heavy, honeyed pulse of primitive need throbbed, swamping every other sense, destroying any chance of thought. Her mouth softened under his, her tongue tangling with his, her sigh a sound of surrender and delight rolled into one.

'Is this what you were looking for, my lady?' Malik muttered against her yielding lips. 'Is this what you wanted?'

'Yes—oh, yes. It's everything I wanted…'

She could barely get the words out, she was so hungry for

his mouth, but even as she reached for him, lacing her arms up and around his strong neck, tangling her fingers in the sleekness of his hair, she heard his husky laughter, raw and deep, low down in his throat.

'Not *everything, sukkar,*' he reproved softly. 'This is very far from everything I can give you.'

And, with a low growl, he caught hold of her, twisted with an easy strength, flipping her over on to her back so that she landed with a soft exclamation on the softness of the cushions, sinking deep into the mattress as Malik came down on top of her, crushing her with his powerful weight.

'So, let's start again…'

He pushed his hands into her hair, holding each side of her head so that she was completely at his mercy, unable to move either to right or left.

'First—a kiss…'

'You've already kissed me…' Abbie tried to protest but Malik shook his head reprovingly.

'A real kiss—the sort of kiss I've been wanting to give you from the first moment that I saw you watching me from that window.'

Unexpectedly and without warning a bubble of laughter rose in Abbie's throat, making her smile up into his dark, intent face.

'In that appalling apron!' she gasped, only to receive a burning glance from those brilliant black eyes, one that told her there was no humour in Malik's mind now, only a primal male need, one that could allow for no resistance, brook no delay.

'In anything,' he told her huskily. 'In anything at all or—preferably—in *nothing* at all. This robe…'

His hands slid down the length of her body, over the silk of the robe, caressing every inch of her, stirring her hunger, building the need for him as the heat of his palms reached pleasure spots that longed for the reality of his touch.

'…is very beautiful, but the truth is that it is nothing like as beautiful as the body beneath it. The silk may be soft but it doesn't compare to the softness of your skin, the satin warmth of your flesh. It may cling to your breasts…'

His hands cupped the swell of her through the fine material, making Abbie gasp aloud in delight and shock at the intensity of the burn of need that shot through her at his touch.

'To your hips…'

Strong fingers smoothed a burning path over her hips and down her thighs, his dark smile growing as he watched her face, felt her writhe in yearning response underneath his imprisoning body.

'And here…'

'Oh—Malik…'

His name broke from her control as one of those tormenting hands cupped the shape of the soft mound between her legs, pressing the fine silk against her sensitised skin, and she saw the burn of an answering need flare in his eyes, sear along the carved cheekbones as he aroused himself as well as her.

'But no silk can ever give me what I want from you. Nothing can compare to the feeling of you, naked and wanting, underneath me, welcoming me, opening to me…'

Those tormenting hands made the return journey back up her body, lingering in the same spots, caressing, tantalising, stirring… Until they were back on either side of her face again, but now they had to hold her still, control the way her head wanted to toss and twist against the silk pillows.

'So first the kiss—here…'

His mouth took hers, hard and strong, giving and demanding in the same moment, forcing her lips open, invading the soft moistness inside, tangling, tasting, teasing…

'And then here…'

This time the heat of his mouth fastened on the tip of one breast where the arousal-hardened nipple pushed against the ivory silk, as if demanding his attention. He suckled her softly through the fine material until the silk was moist and clinging to her skin and the scrape of his teeth sent a stinging arrow of awareness along every nerve, flooding the core of her with heat and hunger.

'Oh, please…please…'

Was she asking him for more—or asking him to stop? In the spinning heat of her mind, Abbie had no idea what she was trying to say, only that *please* was the only word that formed in her thoughts, that her tongue could manage… Please…please…*please.*

'But you are wearing too much—far too much—so this…'

Tanned fingers flicked the crushed and crumpled silk, traced the neckline from the point on her neck where her pulse raced in hungry demand, down to the embroidery-edged opening at the front.

'This has to go…'

And, before she was even aware of what he planned, those powerful hands had caught the two sides of the neckline, gathering the silk up and wrenching it apart, ripping it right down the front until the two sides fell away from her body, leaving her almost totally exposed.

'Malik!'

It was a choking cry of shock, of total disbelief, but he took it as a reproof and shook his head almost violently in rejection.

'It's only a robe,' he told her. 'I will give you another—I will give you a thousand other ones. So long as you're with me, you will never want for clothes—but you will also never want to wear them. Just as you will never want this…'

The scrap of lace that was her bra was swiftly unclipped and tossed aside, hot black eyes feasting on the exposed creamy flesh, the deep pink nipples that stood proud with yearning need.

'Or this…'

Another tug of his hands removed the last of her clothing and he let out a deep, deep sigh of masculine satisfaction as he surveyed her lying there, spread out on the bed, totally naked.

'Now you're as I want you,' he declared, sitting up for a moment to pull his own robe up and over his head, discarding his own underwear before he came back to her, proudly nude, completely unself-conscious in his total male arousal. 'And now we can really begin.'

'B-begin!'

Abbie's mouth trembled on the word, her lips struggling to form it at all. If this was just the beginning then she didn't know how much she could take. But Malik clearly had every intention of taking his time, subjecting her already quivering body to a sensual onslaught that was carefully designed to take her as close to the edge as possible without ever actually pushing her over.

'Do you like this?' he murmured, finding a hundred delicate sensitive spots and using his hands, his mouth, his tongue on them until she was writhing in anguished delight, moaning her pleasure aloud.

'Yes…' she groaned. 'Oh, yessss…'

But Malik shook his head and brought his powerful frame up to straddle her yearning body, long hair-roughened legs on either side of hers, the heated power of his erection pushing into the nest of curls at the centre of her body.

Leaning over her, he took her face in both his hands again, cupping her cheeks, holding her so that she had to look up into his burning eyes.

'I do not understand,' he told her, just the faintest hint of teasing in his thickened voice. 'You have to speak to me in my language—tell me *naam* for yes—*la* for no—then I will be able to do as you want. So…do you like this?'

'*N-naam*…' Abbie sighed.

'And this?'

'*Naam…*'

'And…'

'*Naam…naam…*' Her voice rose until it was almost a scream of ecstasy as his knowing touch sought and found the most intimate, most sensitive place of all and teased it and her into stinging, yearning need. '*Naam!*'

She was clinging to him now, her fingers clenching on the hard, sweat-slicked muscles of his shoulders, nails digging into the bronzed skin. Her body was open to him, arcing towards his in urgent hunger, mutely inviting the fierce invasion that her tongue was incapable of describing in words.

Malik too was beyond speech, his black eyes glazed, his jaw set. But no words were needed, their touch, their kisses did all the communicating that was necessary and as he thrust himself into the moist core of her she gave herself up totally to the sensation of having him there, filling her, stretching her, possessing her.

For a moment the strong body above hers stilled, Malik drawing in a deep, ragged breath as he felt the soft tissues adjust around him. In the silence Abbie heard the air hiss in between his teeth as he struggled for control, for the strength to take the fullest pleasure from the moment, to absorb all it had to offer, to experience it totally. And then, just as she was beginning to fear she might come down from the heated heights to which he had taken her, whimpering in restless protest, he bent his head, kissed her, fierce and hard on her open mouth, and slowly, strongly, began to move.

And with that first moment all the powerful, almost brutal control that he had been exerting broke away from him and splintered irreparably. With a raw cry he gave in to the need he had been denying so long, thrusting in and out, hard and long, letting the wild, primal rhythm take him faster and faster. And Abbie clung to him, her body meeting his, taking his, giving back passion for passion. Together they climbed higher, fiercer, hotter, wilder, until it seemed as if they had broken free of the last threads that held them on the earth and were whirling out of existence and into another, more wonderful, more devastating universe where everything was pure sensation, pure delight. And in that other dimension Abbie lost control completely, dissolved, giving a wild keening cry of sheer fulfilment as she lost herself in a blinding explosion of stars that spun her out of consciousness and into total blank oblivion.

CHAPTER THIRTEEN

In the middle of the night Abbie woke suddenly, unsure of just what had disturbed her. The tent was dark, just one lamp burning in the blackness, and the silence of the desert outside was eerie, completely still.

Beside her, Malik too was still, his breathing soft, his long powerful body relaxed in sleep, the heat from it enclosing her as she lay curled up beside him. A faint smile touched her lips as she remembered the blaze of passion they had shared and she shifted slightly, moving closer so that she could feel his skin against hers, entangle her legs with the muscular strength of his.

And that was when she became aware of the fact that Malik was not actually asleep. He was lying completely still, totally silent, but when she turned her head she saw that he was wide awake and was lying with his head pillowed on his arms folded behind it and he was staring, blank-eyed and un-blinking, up into the draped canopy above him.

And something about his very stillness and the way that those jet-dark eyes were unfocused told her that the thoughts that kept him from sleep were far from happy ones. Instinct led her in the probable direction of the cause.

'Are you thinking about Jalil?' she asked, keeping her voice as soft as possible so that he could act as if he hadn't heard her if that was what he wanted.

But Malik's dark head turned in her direction immediately, the deep-set eyes gleaming in the moonlight as he looked at her.

'I can't believe he's gone,' he said.

Under the covers, Abbie reached for his hand, folded her fingers around it and held tight.

'Would it help to talk? Tell me about him. I only knew the Jalil who was at school with me and then not very well. He was a bit arrogant…'

Malik's mouth twisted into a wry grin and a faint laugh escaped him.

'That's Jalil…that was Jalil,' he adjusted painfully. 'He was the only son—the only child of an elderly father and a doting mother who never denied him anything. Anything he wanted, it was his, and he always expected the rest of the world to treat him the same. He never learned discipline or control but was always lazy, self-indulgent and greedy. That's why he was never very popular with his people…'

His deep sigh made Abbie tighten her grip on the hand she held.

'And that was why he wanted—needed—a wife so much. If he married, had an heir, then things might have settled down a bit.'

'And you'd promised to help him?'

In the darkness Malik's nod was just a movement of the shadows.

'I made a vow to my mother that I would do everything in my power to keep him safe on his throne. In fact, I was the one who told him that marriage was his best hope of stability when there was unrest in Barakhara. At first he refused to listen but then, when things didn't quieten down, he conceded that maybe I had a point. Unfortunately for you, that was the time when your brother decided to help himself to some of the artefacts from the dig. Jalil remembered the crush he had had on you—and he became obsessed with the idea that you were the only bride for him.'

'And you were bound by your promise to help him.'

Under the covers Malik's hand tightened on her own and she felt the warmth of his lips brush her forehead in a gentle acknowledgement of her understanding.

'Bound by it but not in agreement with the way he went about enforcing his wishes. Though I thought it was "Gail" he was blackmailing into being his bride.'

'In Jalil's mind it probably was,' Abbie conceded. 'I was a very different person in those days—I've grown up a lot since.'

'Unfortunately, Jalil had not.'

Malik sighed, pushed his free hand through his hair and pressed it against his temple.

'He was a fool, a selfish, immature fool—but he was my brother.'

'And that bond is so strong that sometimes we have to do things we would never even think of because of it,' Abbie agreed, thinking of Andy. 'My own brother has made some major mistakes too. If he hadn't been so greedy for cash…'

With a rustle of bedclothes, Malik turned towards her and planted another kiss on her mouth.

'Your brother had the misfortune to be *my* brother's means to an end. If Jalil hadn't wanted to have you as his wife, then he might well have been more prepared to listen to reason where Andy was concerned.'

In the concealing darkness the effect of that kiss was more than doubled, the taste of Malik's lips on hers intensified, the warm musky scent of his body reaching her as he stirred, the sound of his softly accented voice like music in the stillness of the night. Already the heat of need was lapping at her senses, making her far from satiated body come to life.

But there was something in the back of her mind that needed saying. Some question she still needed answering if she could just get her thoughts to work on it.

'How come Jalil needed an heir so badly and you don't? I mean, isn't it slightly hypocritical of you to have insisted that he did his duty by his country when you were still foot-loose and fancy free? After all, you're so much older than him and there isn't even a sign of a wife in your life.'

Except me... a small voice whispered in reminder inside her head but she pushed it away hastily. She couldn't quite believe that Malik had ever meant that sudden and impulsive offer of marriage, and if she was honest just at this moment she didn't even care. She had dreamed of being with the man she loved for at least one night of her life, and that dream had been fulfilled. In fact, she was still living out that dream and she was wasting precious time *talking* when they could be doing something much more pleasurable.

Besides, she knew the answer to her own question. Malik would never have let his country come close to rebellion because of his own behaviour. He would always have had a far stronger hold on the reins of power than his brother.

'Of course I need an heir,' Malik surprised her by answering. It was a shock to feel his breath on her face as he spoke. 'And I need one more than ever now that I've inherited Jalil's throne and have two kingdoms to rule over.'

When had he come so much closer? She could feel the length of his body pressed up against hers and the heat and strength of his obvious arousal pushed into the softness of her belly as a result.

'The fact is that I was once about to be married but it never actually happened—she had an unrecognised heart weakness and she died a few months before the wedding was to take place.'

'I'm sorry...'

She could feel the rasp of his day's growth of beard as she spoke, her lips almost pressed against the planes of his cheek, the line of his strong jaw.

'Don't be—except for her. It was an arranged marriage. I hardly knew her.'

But he would have married her, would have had children with her.

'You didn't love her?'

'Love didn't come into it. It wasn't important.'

And there she had her own fate declared in that flat, emotionless statement.

Even if he had meant the proposal he had flung at her—a proposal forced from him as much by the shocking events of the day as from any real belief in what he was offering—then he couldn't have made it any plainer that what he was looking for in a marriage was not emotional commitment.

Love…wasn't important.

So could she live with him—marry him—spend the rest of her life with him on those terms? Could she accept the little he would offer her emotionally and let it be enough?

'Marriage, your brother's freedom—a life of luxury beyond your wildest imaginings—and every night of your life spent in my bed…'

Malik's words, flung at her in the heat and despair of the moment, came back to torment her, echoing cruelly inside her head. He had thought that he was offering her so much, but the truth was that for her it was far too little.

Malik might be able to offer her huge wealth, a life of luxury, but how could it ever be enough when she wanted, needed, longed for him to love her as she loved him?

'What is important?' she managed to whisper, fighting to wipe the tone of bitter disappointment from her words and hoping, praying, that he might just possibly say something more than what she already knew.

But her silent prayer went unanswered.

'What's important?' Malik murmured, coming even closer and enfolding her in the strength of his arms, 'Oh, *sukkar*, do you even have to ask? This is important…'

He drifted kisses over her hair, her forehead, over the closed lids of her eyes.

'And this…'

His hands began to move over her body, stroking, caressing, tantalising, finding the spots that were still needy, even after his attentions earlier in the night, stirring them, rousing them, making her writhe in growing response. Her mouth opened willingly to his, her tongue tangling in an intimate dance with his, and as the fire invaded her body she knew that, for now at least, she didn't, couldn't, care.

For now, Malik was right—this was important and she was not going to spoil it with thoughts about the future or worries about what might be.

For now, this was important—because it might be all she would ever have. This primal, fierce passion might be the only thing that Malik would ever feel for her, and right now that made it the most important and the most wonderful thing in all the world.

It was a long time before Malik's heart stopped racing, before his breathing eased. But as he slowly came back to himself he found himself wishing that he could have stayed in the mindless unconsciousness of the sexual force that had swamped him several times during the night.

At least there he had known what he was doing. He had known what he felt—and he had had a damn good idea of what Abbie was feeling too. Now, as the heated delirium ebbed from his mind and his body, he saw how little they had actually resolved. If anything.

'This marriage that you're offering…' Abbie had said. 'Show me what it would be like—and then I'll decide.'

And he'd shown her.

He'd shown himself too. He could hardly believe the experience he'd just had. Couldn't find the words to describe it, even to himself. He'd been taken out of this world and into another, a place he'd never known existed. And now that he was back in reality he knew that he would do anything—everything in his power to repeat that experience again and again.

Which meant keeping Abbie in his life.

A faint sound from the woman at his side made him turn, look down at her. She was still asleep, her long limbs relaxed and at ease, her breathing deep, her long tangled hair falling forward over her face. With a gentle hand he moved the blonde strands from her face and studied it silently.

Any minute now she would wake and tell him her decision. But there was only one decision he wanted to hear.

He had wanted this woman from the moment he had seen her. And last night had only added to that hunger, rather than doing anything to appease it. He no longer cared if she was only interested in him because of his wealth and power. She could be the worst gold-digger in the world and he would still want her. He couldn't lose her. Now that he had her, he would keep her whatever it took.

'Malik…?'

She was waking, stirring, stretching. Every movement of her body stirred his senses, made desire twist deep inside, setting his pulse racing again, his breathing becoming raw and uneven. All he wanted to do was to reach for, drag her into his arms, kiss her senseless…

But that was only a temporary solution. An immensely satisfying, intensely pleasurable temporary solution, but a short-lived, transient one all the same. He wanted more than that and so he was going to have to play this another way. So, in spite of the fact that it positively *hurt* to do it, he forced himself from the bed, snatched up his robe, and pulled it on just as Abbie stirred again, her heavy eyes opening slowly, blinking sleepily.

'Malik?'

Noticing his absence immediately, she pushed herself up on the cushions, turning her head sharply, blonde hair flying, looking for him in the grey light of dawn that was filtering into the tent.

'What are you doing? Where are you going?' she demanded when she saw that he was dressing.

'We're leaving.'

Was he fooling himself or had there been just the faintest reaction to that 'we'? Had she really thought that he would go without her? That he would leave her behind?

'Going where?'

'To Edhan—to my palace. We have a wedding—our wedding—to arrange.'

'Our wedding? But…'

She was obviously about to fling back the bedclothes and get out, coming to remonstrate with him, but an attack of second thoughts made her pause and decide to stay where she was.

'But I never said…'

'You didn't have to.'

Malik stamped his feet into soft leather boots, snatching up his cloak from the pile of cushions on to which he had tossed it the previous night.

'Your reaction last night said everything there was to say.'

Knowing it was coming, he watched the flare of indignation blaze in her eyes, saw the way that smooth, defiant chin came up, her soft mouth firming.

'I…' she began, but he had no intention of letting her finish.

'"This marriage that you're offering—with every night of my life spent in your bed,"' he quoted at her harshly, not wanting to give her an inch. '"Show me what it would be like—and then I'll decide." I showed you…' he added when she opened her mouth to argue. 'I showed you what it was—what it *is* going to be like, and now I see no point at all in wasting any time. We're going to Edhan and we're going to be married.'

She was about to argue again so he covered the space between them in a couple of swift, determined strides, taking that rebellious chin in his hand and holding it just where he wanted it as he planted a swift, silencing kiss on her partly open mouth.

'So I suggest you get up and get dressed, unless you plan on riding all the way to the capital dressed—or rather undressed—like that.'

And while she was still spluttering with indignation, still trying to find a way to answer him, he turned on his heel and marched out into the cool of early morning, letting the tent flap fall closed behind him, muffling her furious shout of his name.

CHAPTER FOURTEEN

Marriage, your brother's freedom—a life of luxury beyond your wildest imaginings...

The words ran round and round on a never-ending loop inside Abbie's head all day, every day, from the moment that she woke up until the moment she fell asleep. And if she woke at any point in the night too, they were still there, still reminding her of how much Malik had promised her—and how little.

The luxury beyond her wildest imaginings was always there in the huge palace with its marble floors and walls, the decorations picked out in gold, the crystal chandeliers everywhere. There were miles and miles of corridors, huge ornately furnished rooms, and the suite allocated to her was enormous, bigger even than the flat she had once shared with three friends when she had been at university.

She had servants to attend to every possible need—and a few that she hadn't even realised she had. It seemed as if she had only to think of something and it was hers, sometimes without ever asking for it or raising her hand to indicate what she needed.

The cases that she had packed when she had thought that she was going to meet Jalil had been delivered and carefully unpacked and placed in the huge wardrobes where they had looked a little lost amongst all the hanging space. But then that space hadn't been there for long as Malik had ordered a vast wardrobe of new clothes for her, western designer outfits together with an endless range of traditional clothing, robes in the finest silks, in a hundred different colours, hand embroidered with beautiful designs. There were jewels too, necklaces and bracelets, ornate earrings in gold and set with the finest stones money could buy.

And in her wardrobe hung one very special gown with its matching robe, crafted from pure white silk, embroidered with silver and gold and with a matching scarf for her hair, so fine that it looked like a spider's web spun from pure gold.

Her wedding gown.

Because it was obvious that Malik was determined that the marriage was going ahead.

From the moment that he had walked out of their tent and started issuing orders to prepare for their journey back to Edhan, he had blithely ignored any attempt she had made to protest that she hadn't actually agreed to his proposal, that at no time had she ever said that she would be his bride.

'I showed you what it is going to be like,' he'd declared, 'and now I see no point at all in wasting any time. We're going to Edhan and we're going to be married.'

And here they were in the palace in Edhan, and preparations were well under way. No one could accuse him of wasting any time about it! The wedding was to be held at the end of the week—just five days from now—and less than a fortnight since she had left the oasis encampment and travelled back here to this city, this country where Malik was ruler of all he surveyed.

Privately Abbie wished they could still be in that oasis, in the small black tent under the desert stars where everything had seemed so simple and so possible. The single night she had spent there in Malik's arms held a magical memory for her as the one night when she had known the heat and the passion of his loving in a way that was wild enough and powerful enough to drive away all the fears and doubts that had clouded her mind. In that tent, Malik had just been a man and she had just been a woman and the sensual fires they had built between them had held the world at bay at least for the length of that glorious night.

Now they were back in the world and Malik was a different man. A sheikh. A ruler now of not one but two different countries. He had had to arrange Jalil's funeral, and then he had so many things to do and so little time to spare that she barely saw him, even at night.

If she could at least have shared his bed then she might have been able to talk to him, or try to burn away her doubts in the heat of the sexual desire they felt for each other. But she slept alone in the huge, softly comfortable bed in the private suite she had been given, too often lying awake, staring at the ornate patterns of arches and mosaics that formed the ceiling above her.

Marriage, your brother's freedom—a life of luxury beyond your wildest imaginings...

Your brother's freedom...

And there was one other reason why she didn't dare to go to Malik and tell him that she didn't think she could marry him after all.

Andy.

Malik had promised that he would free Andy and he had kept his word. In fact, he had acted far more quickly than she had ever anticipated. On the very same day that they arrived at the palace in Edhan, Abbie's brother had been freed from the jail where he was imprisoned and brought to the palace, where he was reunited with his sister. He was here now, along with her parents and a stunned, bug-eyed George who had seen as many camels as his heart desired, ready to attend the wedding ceremony when it took place.

When she had first seen him, Abbie had been appalled by Andy's thinness and pallor but after a few days of freedom, of relaxation and proper food, he was finally starting to fill out, to look more human. But that improvement was dependent on him being out of prison and being properly looked after.

And his freedom was dependent on her marrying Malik.

So, in spite of her fears, she had to go through with this.

She could do this, Abbie told herself. She had to do it. She had no choice.

She even managed to convince herself until Malik had stunned her by introducing her to his best friend's wife.

'Lucy has been through all this herself,' he told her when he announced that Sheikh Hakim bin Taimur Al Fulani and his English wife, the former Lucy Mannion, were coming to stay for a few days before the wedding ceremony. 'She and Hakim have only been married a year, so she knows all about the problems of adjusting—she'll help you with the problems and the possible pitfalls you might encounter. I also think you'll like her—you could become friends.'

Abbie had thought so too. Lucy, a petite blonde, very close to her own age, was a delightful person, someone she found it easy to get to know and even easier to like. Under any other circumstances, she would have enjoyed the other girl's company and welcomed her help with the complicated and stressful preparations for the approaching royal wedding.

But these weren't anything like normal circumstances. For one thing she, Abbie, was preparing for a wedding that she hadn't really ever said yes to. And for another, Lucy's presence and her obvious deeply loving relationship with her new husband, Hakim, threw the fake relationship that Abbie had with Malik into sharp relief, revealing it for the pretence that it was.

From the moment of Lucy's arrival at the palace, Abbie's doubts, already disturbing enough, took even deeper root, growing worse and worse with every day that passed. But the final straw was when Lucy, obviously bursting to tell someone, whispered a secret to her newfound friend.

'I'm pregnant, Abbie,' she said, barely able to get the words out for the width of her smile. 'I just found out I'm having Hakim's baby in seven months' time.'

'That's wonderful!' Abbie managed a genuine smile back. She was truly delighted for Lucy and her charming husband.

But her struggle for inward composure was shattered completely when Lucy added, 'You and Malik will have to hurry up and start a family too and then our little ones can grow up together.'

If anything was guaranteed to destroy Abbie's ability to think straight then that was it.

There was a long ceremonial banquet as part of the wedding celebrations and simply sitting through it was an endurance test for her. She had to sit beside Malik, devastatingly handsome in his traditional robes, and watch him receive the congratulations, the good wishes of what seemed like hundreds of guests. Never before had this man she loved seemed so outrageously exotic and arrogantly masculine. Never before had he looked so gloriously striking, so wonderfully attractive, and she found it impossible to do more than pick at her meal and swallow the smallest sips of her drink as she watched him with loving eyes.

Loving but lost eyes.

Because Lucy's words had reminded her of the part of this arrangement that she had been desperately trying to forget. Marriage was more than just two people living together, making love together. As far as Malik was concerned, that making love was for a purpose—and the purpose was to get himself an heir.

'Of course I need an heir,' he'd said. 'And I need one more than ever now that I've inherited Jalil's throne and have two kingdoms to rule over.'

Could she really go ahead with this marriage, knowing that Malik would expect a child from her to be his much-needed heir? It was one thing committing herself to a man who didn't love her when she felt she had no choice, but was it right to create a child from that marriage, knowing that the baby's father had never loved its mother?

Malik would see no wrong in it. He had been planning on an arranged marriage from the start, would have been married to his first chosen bride if she hadn't died so tragically. He would have no problem in going ahead with the marriage—and with fatherhood—this way.

But could she justify it to herself?

'Are you not well?'

Malik had noticed Abbie's silence, the way the colour had faded from her face. She had barely touched her meal, but had simply pushed the food around on her plate, putting very little of it near her mouth.

Her smile was swift, brief and a little wan, fading rapidly at the edges before it really had time to form.

'I'm just a little tired,' she murmured, her grey eyes dropping away from his concerned scrutiny. 'I—haven't been sleeping too well.'

'A strange bed and unaccustomed surroundings.' Malik nodded. 'And there has been so much to plan and prepare...'

Leaning forward, he took her hand, looking deeply into her cloudy eyes.

'And I have been neglectful of you lately.'

'You've had so much to do.'

'True—but that is no excuse. You are my betrothed—my bride-to-be. I should not be so inattentive to you. It is wrong.'

With a small, gentle tug on her hands he drew her even closer until he could rest his cheek against the softness of her skin and whisper right in her delicate ear.

'Shall I come to you tonight, *habibti*? Shall I share your bed—help you to sleep? I am sure that you would rest more easily in my arms.'

For a moment he thought she was actually going to refuse. Her eyes dropped to stare down at their linked hands and white teeth worried at the pink softness of her lower lip.

She couldn't say no! He would die if she held back now—if she said she wanted to sleep alone. Not that sleeping was what he was thinking of. He had found the nights' separation from her as difficult as she so obviously had. But he'd been working long days and long hours into the night and he had left her alone so as not to disturb her. The wedding day would come soon enough and when the ceremonies were over they would have all the rest of their lives together.

Tonight she looked lovelier than ever. Dressed in a silk gown that almost exactly matched her eyes and with her shimmering blonde hair piled up on the top of her head, diamonds at her ears and throat, she was incandescently beautiful, a pale ethereal vision of delight.

'Abbie…?' he prompted when she hesitated.

He'd missed her more than he could imagine and at this moment, with the scent of her body blended with some soft floral perfume tormenting his nostrils, he could barely control the hunger that was clutching at him. It was all he could do to stay in his seat and not leap to his feet, snatch her up and carry her off to his rooms, to his bed, right there and then.

'Yes…' she said at last and it was only when his breath hissed out between his teeth that he realised how much he had been holding it in and for how long. 'Yes, I'd like that.'

Like! In Malik's ears the word sounded too insipid, too restrained to match the way he was feeling. But then he was forgetting that Abbie was a fine-bred English woman and that restraint, in language at least, had probably been drummed into her from birth. But he knew from glorious experience that the one place his fine English wife-to-be entirely lost her grip on those reins of restraint was in bed.

In public now, with her cool colouring, her pale hair, her cool silver dress and the diamonds he had given her sparkling like ice around her neck and in her lobes, she might look like a water spirit, calm and clear as liquid. But when she was in bed with him, under him, opening to him, then she was all fire and air, as wild and wanton as any man's dream of a woman would be.

And tonight he would be with her again.

'Wait for me,' he told her softly, fighting to keep his voice level, his breathing even. The images his thoughts had thrown up at him were so powerfully erotic, so furiously arousing that he was going to have to struggle for control for the rest of the evening.

But that struggle would be all the more worthwhile when he finally joined this woman—his woman—in her bed. Then he would throw off all the constraints he had been fighting against and lose himself completely in her welcoming body.

The time couldn't come soon enough.

Somehow he managed to get through the hours that remained until he was free. He spoke with the right people, thanked the ones he needed to thank, accepted congratulations until his head was buzzing with them. And then, at long last, everyone had retired to bed, the palace was silent, the lights turned off in all but the most personal quarters, and he could go to Abbie.

To the woman who was soon to be his wife.

He hadn't felt this way since he had been an adolescent, escaping the confines of school, the palace, and saddling his favourite Arabian stallion, heading out into the wilds of the country, riding free with the desert wind in his hair. But tonight he didn't need to leave the palace to escape.

Tonight he had everything he needed right here.

He prayed she would still be waiting for him. She had never regained any of the colour in her face and had escaped the banquet at the earliest possible opportunity, pleading tiredness. Perhaps that tiredness would have overcome her and she had fallen asleep. Even just thinking of it made his body tense in anticipated frustration.

But then… As he had learned in one night, in a tent in the desert, there was a whole new sort of satisfaction to be found in just lying beside a woman, holding her close and watching her sleep.

At least there was that satisfaction with *this* woman. It was something he had never known with any other woman who had shared his bed. And the moment when she stirred, woke, opened her eyes and looked up into his face, with her silvery gaze still blurred from sleep, her expression soft, her mouth just the tiniest bit open…

Damn it! He was too hard, too hot already to even *think* about that. He couldn't even pause to discard the ornate ceremonial robes and change into something much more simple. He didn't want to waste a single second.

Let her be waiting for him… Please let her be waiting!

She was.

At the first glance into the room, where only a single bedside lamp burned to lighten the darkness, he thought that she had given him up. But then, as his eyes adjusted to the gloom, he saw that there was no sign of anyone in the bed, and in a faint pool of light he caught the gleam of her fair hair where she was sitting in a chair by the window.

She had discarded the gown she had worn for the banquet, pulling on a white silk robe that was wrapped around her slender form, knotted at the narrow waist. But her hair was still piled up on top of her head and the diamond necklace and earrings still glinted against her pale skin. She looked like an ice maiden—an ice queen.

An ice queen who would very soon turn to fire in his arms.

'Abbie!'

Barely pausing to kick the door to behind him, he crossed the room in half a dozen swift strides, his arms already reaching for her as he approached. And she rose to meet him, coming up out of her chair and almost throwing herself into those outstretched arms, with his name a cry of welcome on her lips. Their bodies met, mouths fused, hands grabbed and clung.

She was wearing nothing under the white robe. He could feel that from the way her breasts swung unfettered against his chest, the smooth sleek line of her hips and buttocks with not even the finest hint of lace to conceal, to mar the perfection of her skin.

And the robe itself was no barrier to his urgent hands. In seconds he had wrenched open the tie belt, ripped the silk from her body and, sweeping her off her feet and up into his arms, he carried her to the bed, flung her down. Discarding his own clothing with a violent haste, he came down beside her on the silken cover.

'I have been waiting for this so long.'

'Then you don't have to wait any longer.'

She was reaching for him even as she whispered the words, her soft hands closing over his arms, drawing her to him, her legs already parting underneath him, offering herself, giving herself, inviting him in. And she was already so soft, so wet, so obviously hungry for him too that he barely hesitated long enough to draw a heaving breath before he thrust into her, hearing her moan of sensual response as her yearning body lifted to meet his, her inner muscles closing round him.

It was hard, it was fierce, it was demanding. It was hot as hell. So hot that there was no chance at all of lingering, of delaying, of giving. It was all he could do not to let himself go in the first few glorious seconds. But Abbie didn't seem to want delay, or even finesse. Lying there beneath him like some wild tribal queen, naked except for the brilliant glitter of the jewels she wore, she urged him on with soft little groans and louder cries, her nails digging into the flesh on his back, her mouth nipping at his lips, his face, his chest. And when she gave a final, wicked little twist of her hips, taking all control from him as she slid herself up and down his throbbing shaft, he lost all control completely and gave himself up to the explosion that rocked his senses to their core.

'Abbie—my wife—my queen...'

It escaped him on a raw cry of rapture and somewhere in the shattered remnants of his mind he heard her answering whimper of delight, the keening moan of the moment of release as they both lost themselves in the blazing consummation of mindless ecstasy.

Malik thought that his heart had stopped completely. The next moment he believed that his pulse would never stop racing, that his breathing would never, ever settle down again. His head spun, his hands shook—his whole body shook. He had never known anything like it.

He had been taken out of the existence he knew, caught up in a whirlwind and a firestorm combined, hurled higher than he had ever been—and dropped back down to earth in a world that could never be the same again.

The one thing he knew was that Abbie was there with him—and Abbie was all he needed, all he wanted. All he had been looking for all his life.

'Abbie...'

He lifted his head from where it had fallen on to her shoulder as he'd collapsed on top of her, with his face crushed up against the hardness of the necklace, the jewels digging into his cheek.

'Abbie...' It was all he could manage as he pressed his lips against her face... And jolted upright, forced out of the sensual haze into which he had drifted by the taste of salt, the feel of moisture under his mouth.

'Tears? Abbie, *habibti*—why?'

Why? Oh, dear heaven, how did she ever answer that?

Released from the imprisoning pressure of Malik's long body, Abbie rolled over on to her side to curl in a miserable heap, her face and the betraying tears hidden in the cover.

She had never meant to dissolve into tears. She had been determined to be strong, to cope with this in the best way she could.

Waiting in the darkness for Malik to come to her, she had reached a decision, one that threatened to break her heart, but one that she knew was the only way forward for her.

She couldn't marry Malik, couldn't live with him for the rest of her life, loving him and knowing that he didn't love her. It would destroy her, take her heart and rip it to shreds. And when she added the thought that she might have a baby, a child who needed, deserved, two parents who loved each other, she had known that her decision had been made for her.

She had resolved that she would tell him tonight—but first she would allow herself the private personal indulgence of one more—one last chance to make love with him.

It would hurt, it would be a bitter-sweet experience, and she had been prepared for that. What she hadn't been ready for was the wild, fierce, totally overwhelming, all-consuming tidal wave of passion that had swamped her. The waves of love and need had broken over her head, swamping her, drowning her, taking her up and up into the greatest ecstasy she had ever known...

...And then she had been dropped right down on to the barren shore once more, knowing it was over and she would never experience such joy again.

And that was when the tears had come, flowing down her cheeks in rivulets of misery that she just couldn't even try to control.

'Abbie...'

Malik's hand on her shoulder was gentle, his voice soft, concerned.

'Why the tears? Why are you crying?'

Sniffing inelegantly, swiping at her face with the back of her hand, Abbie couldn't meet his searching gaze.

'I—we—Lucy's pregnant.'

'She is?'

It was clearly the last thing he had been expecting and his proud head went back in shock.

'She is? Hakim will be overjoyed. But...'

To Abbie's horror, he touched her again, turning her face towards him.

'Why is this a cause for sadness? Surely celebrations are—'

Tears flooded her eyes again so that his handsome face was just a blur.

'Celebrations for them perhaps—but what if we...?'

'You don't want children?' Malik jumped to the wrong conclusion when the words were choked off in her constricted throat, impossible to take any further. 'Abbie, if that's a problem then you only have to say. We don't have to have a baby if it's the last thing you want.'

The last thing... It was the thing she most wanted in all the world, if only it had been possible—if Malik only loved her.

'But—but you need an heir.'

She had to get a grip on herself or she would never be able to do this. Pushing herself up into a sitting position, she grabbed at a pillow and wiped her eyes on it, blinking hard to clear the stinging moisture from her vision. Then, pulling out a sheet from under her, she tugged it up, creating a fragile, partially protective wrap that at least concealed, even if it wasn't enough to act as any sort of armour against the pain.

'I need an heir,' Malik told her, looking deep into her tear-stained eyes. 'But if you don't—then when we marry—'

And this was when she had to say it. She had hoped that the moment wouldn't come so soon, that she would have a little time at least to prepare herself. To find the words she needed, but it seemed that the Fates were not going to be so kind.

And still, perhaps it was so much better this way. If she could just get it said and done and over with then maybe—

maybe—she might have the chance to get away and lick her wounds in private. Not to recover, because she was sure that she never would recover from this. Would never recover from loving Malik and knowing that she could have been his but he would never, ever be hers.

'We aren't going to marry,' she said as firmly as she could manage with her throat closing tight over the words, her breathing raw and agonising in her lungs. 'That's just the point, Malik. I can't do this. I won't marry you.'

'You won't…'

It was Malik's turn to rear back, his eyes narrowing in instant shock and disbelief. The movement freed the rest of the sheet that Abbie was wrapped in enough to let her off the bed, hauling the white linen with her and wrapping it around her further, toga-style. The concealing folds gave her a little more courage to go on.

'I won't marry you. I know you thought I was going to. You believed that I accepted your proposal—but I never did.'

'I offered you…'

'I know—I know about Andy. You freed him because of our arrangement, because I said I'd marry you, but please, please don't send him back to prison. I'll take his place—I'll serve his sentence…'

'You would rather go to prison than marry me? Don't be bloody stupid, woman!'

It was a wild, ferocious roar. The fury of a desert ruler thwarted by a mere commoner, and a woman at that.

'Your brother has nothing to do with this! Nothing! And he is most definitely not going back to prison—and nor are you. I was going to free him anyway—no matter what you said to my proposal of marriage.'

'He—you…'

Abbie couldn't get her breath back enough to speak.

'You were going to free him?'

'Of course. He's been a fool but, he assures me he didn't know the things he took had any religious significance and I believe him. Whatever he did, he certainly didn't deserve the sentence Jalil imposed on him.'

'But you said…'

'Your brother's freedom was part of what I was offering you in marriage—it wasn't there only *on condition* you married me. Andy is free—and he'll stay free, no matter what happens between us.'

'Thank you.'

It was all that she could manage.

'Thank you with all my heart,' she tried to go on, but Malik ignored her.

'So now that we have the suspicion of blackmailing you into marriage out of the way—will you please reconsider your decision not to marry me?'

That 'please' almost destroyed her but she had to hold strong.

'I can't.'

For a few terrible seconds she thought that he was going to argue. That he was going to refuse to accept her declaration. But then his face closed up, shutters coming down behind the black eyes, and he pushed himself off the bed, stalking across the room to snatch up the black robe he had discarded in such haste just a heartbreakingly few moments before. Slinging it on, he pulled the gaping front together over his chest, folding his arms to hold it secure, and the way that this man, normally so proud and totally unembarrassed by his nudity, had covered himself spoke volumes for the way he was feeling.

'You can't do this,' he said, cold and proud and totally autocratic. 'I won't allow it.'

'Oh, Malik—' Abbie sighed '—I have to. I've thought and thought about this and it's the only answer I can come up with—the only thing to do. I know all the reasons why you'll think that the wedding can't be cancelled, but I've thought them through and it can be done. It'll be inconvenient, but…'

'What reasons?' Malik demanded, shocking her with the savage ferocity of his tone. 'What reasons, Abbie? Tell me the reasons why it will be so *inconvenient* to cancel our marriage.'

'Why—well—the invitations have been sent out, the dignitaries are starting to arrive, the robes have been made…'

'The feasts are ordered, the decorations planned.' Malik took up the list in a tone so brutally cold that it made her toes curl in horror on the hard marble floor. 'I have your father's blessing, I've given you jewels—the bridal gift…'

'I know…'

With shaking hands, she reached up to unfasten the necklace, remove the dangling earrings from her lobes. Hurriedly she moved towards him, holding out the hand that held the jewellery.

'And now I'm giving them back to you. I don't want them—and you'll need these for the woman you marry—for your real bride.'

Malik glanced down at the sparkling handful, just once. Then, in a gesture of total disdain, he snatched at her fingers, folded them back over the brilliant jewels, thrust it back at her.

'Keep them,' he snarled. 'I gave them to you. I will never give them to any other woman, because if you do not marry me then I will never take another wife. There is no other woman I could ever meet who I'd want to marry after you.'

'Malik, please… I know how you—how we both feel—but sexual desire isn't the foundation to build a marriage upon.'

'Sexual desire?' Malik dismissed her protest with an arrogant wave of his hand. 'Desire isn't all of it. It isn't the only reason I want to marry you. The real reason is the one you've missed off your list of *inconveniences*. It's the reason you've forgotten, or perhaps that you didn't know—the most important reason of all.'

'And that is?'

She had no idea what he was going to say—didn't even dare begin to guess because the wild flames she saw in his eyes told her that it was more than important—that it was something so vital to Malik that he had no way of concealing how he felt.

'That I love you—that you are my dream, my soul mate, my life. I love you more than the world and that is why I want to marry you. That is why I can't cancel this wedding, because the truth is that I think I will die if I have to—that I can't go on if I'm forced to live without you.'

'Oh, Malik…'

Tears of joy slid from the corners of her eyes as she struggled to believe she had heard right, struggled to accept that all her dreams had come true. That this man she loved—adored—with all her heart loved her back with all the power and strength of which he was capable.

'Malik…'

She fought back the tears, blinking hard so that she could see his beloved face in this most important moment in her life.

'I love you too, but I thought you would never care for me—that's why I felt I couldn't go through with our marriage.'

'Not care for you?'

Malik's laugh had such a raw, shaken edge to it that it caught on her heart and tugged it painfully.

'Oh, Abbie, I once thought that I could accept an arranged marriage—a marriage that would bring me the heirs I needed, the security for my country. But as I got to know you I realised that I'd just been deceiving myself to think that I could live that way. I wanted you, needed you. Any woman in the world could give me the children I need—but only one woman on earth could be my true *wife*—the centre of my world. My reason for living.'

To Abbie's stunned amazement, he took her hand in his, then sank to one knee on the polished marble floor, looking up into her bemused face with intent jet-black eyes.

'Let's start again and do this right, this time. Abbie, my life, love, will you marry me and be my queen—the queen of my country—of my world—for the rest of our lives?'

Abbie had to swallow hard to relieve the tight constriction in her throat, to enable her to find the words to answer him. She could hardly believe that this was Malik, the Sheikh, the desert ruler. He'd swept into her room like the proud, arrogant king he was, dressed in ceremonial robes, his head high, black eyes filled with all the pride of his lineage. But now he was kneeling at her feet with all that pride, that arrogance, royalty stripped from him.

There was only Malik the man, laid bare for her as he would do for no other person in the world.

He was waiting for her answer.

And there was only one answer she could give him.

Folding her hand around his, she lowered herself to the floor beside him, kneeling as close to him as she could manage as she held his black, questioning gaze with her steady, glowing silver one.

'Yes, my darling Malik,' she told him softly but confidently, no trace of doubt putting even the hint of hesitation into her voice. 'Yes, my king. I will marry you and be your queen—and love you with all my heart.'

And, leaning forward into his waiting arms, she sealed her vow with a long, loving kiss.

HARLEQUIN *Presents*

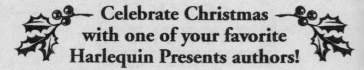

**Celebrate Christmas
with one of your favorite
Harlequin Presents authors!**

THE SICILIAN'S CHRISTMAS BRIDE

by Sandra Marton

On sale November 2006.

When Maya Sommers becomes Dante Russo's
mistress, rules are made. Although their affair
will be highly satisfying in the bedroom,
there'll be no commitment or future plans.
Then Maya discovers she's pregnant....

Get your copy today!